RENEGADE

Little
DOZEN
pre

RENEGADE

BOOK 4 OF THE ONENESS CYCLE

by Rachel Starr Thomson

Little Dozen Press

2015

"And the LORD heard it; and his anger was kindled; and the fire of the LORD burnt among them, and consumed them . . . And he called the name of the place Taberah: because the fire of the LORD burnt among them."
—Numbers 11:1, 3

"And others save with fear, pulling them out of the fire."
—Jude 1:23

The woods around the cabin were deep and dark—the kind of place that was perfect for filming low-budget horror movies. Or for facing real demons.

For Reese, it was the perfect setting for the game of cat-and-mouse she found herself in.

Crouching beneath a short ledge in the rocky terrain, with the roots of a pine spilling over the side and plunging back into the ground all around her, she waited in the half-light for the thing to come closer. She had split her weight between the ledge at her back and one leg. The other leg, swathed in a heavy ankle cast, was stretched out before her.

She could see the hunter moving in the treed shadows before her—movement like a spider picking its way slowly through the obstacles of the woods. It was coming after her physically, so it had chosen a body. A real spider? She wasn't sure. Demons often caused the bodies of their hosts to grow, but this would be impressive beyond anything she had seen before. It was huge—easily twice her height.

She was glad Tyler and Jacob were back at the cabin. She hadn't told them about the hunters.

Her sword rested lightly in her hand, as much a part of her as her own limbs. Right now, with the creature a clear shot in front her, bow and arrows might be handier. But that had never been Reese's style.

Her heart beat a little faster as she waited for the demon to close in. She was banking on it being alone—that nothing would come at her from behind or beside. She just needed it to close the distance between them—to pounce.

It stepped into a shaft of light between the heavier woods and the ridge. Stared right at her, yellow insect eyes glaring. It was a spider—and it wasn't. She had never seen anything like it. Had it somehow managed to merge two hosts?

The monster before her had eight arachnoid limbs and four eyes that were not those of a mammal, but its body and head were like those of a wolf. In the city, where she was used to fighting demons, demons didn't take such creative forms.

But this was better than fighting a human host any day.

"Come on," she said quietly. "What are you waiting for?"

The demon regarded her without moving. Its entire body reverberated with tension, ready for the leap.

She stared at it, equally still, equally tensed. This was a duel, pistol to pistol, the only questions those of nerve, aim, and timing.

It leaped.

Spider arms, sharp on their ends, skewered the ridge on every side of her. She twisted the sword, buried deep in its abdomen,

Rachel Starr Thomson

and wished she could close her ears against its shrieks. The body shrivelled as the demon fled.

She pulled the sword free of the shrunken form, breathing hard.

Before her lay a dead wolf. The arachnoid arms and eyes had disappeared, gone with the demon spirit that had animated the monster.

With a grunt, she pushed herself up on her cramping muscles and reached for the crutch on the ridge behind her.

This was the fourth hunter she had dispatched in two days. She didn't know why they were after her or how they knew where to look. It was strange for demons to be abroad in a place like this—in the forest, far away from the human evils they usually fed off of.

She wiped sweat from her brow and started her limping way back to the cabin. Her sword had smoothly disappeared—there were no more demons in the area. For now.

Why me? she asked the air. And why now?

In the old days, if something like this had happened she would have gone straight to her cell to ask for help, both in understanding what was going on and in combating it.

Straight to David, their cell leader, who had betrayed her.

She didn't have a cell anymore. She knew the group from the village would claim her as their own—already did, in fact. They had welcomed her and made their home hers. But her own inner wounds and Jacob's claims had turned her world further upside down than she'd known was possible, and until she had answers, she couldn't return their embrace.

So she was alone, fighting off the creatures who were tracking her and trying to make sense of their attacks even as she hid the struggle from Tyler and Jacob and hoped they would leave the cabin soon. Coming here was Jacob's plan. This was another of his old haunts, and he was waiting for something that he expected to happen while they were here—she didn't know what. But she needed healing, for her ankle if not her heart, so she complied. In any case, this mountain area was much like her childhood home, and coming back here almost felt like she could find a new start.

In the meantime, Jacob told stories every night in the cabin. Stories that drove home his life's thesis: that the Oneness had to stop fighting their battle on a spiritual plane alone and take it into the real, physical, human world.

Easy for him to say, Reese thought. He wasn't fighting off demonic trackers every time he was alone.

She came in sight of the cabin and sighed. A small log house with a couple of bunks and a stove—really little more than a hut—it had been home for the last week. A temporary sanctuary while she couldn't go anywhere that was actually home.

Tyler was sitting out front, whittling a branch with a rusted knife he'd found in the desk inside the cabin.

"Hey," he said, looking up as Reese approached. "Out for a hike?"

"Yeah."

"Can't be easy with your ankle."

Reese laid her crutches aside and lowered herself beside him, using the cabin wall to steady herself. "It isn't. But the ankle's healing."

Tyler nodded. "Good." He frowned. "You okay? You look like you just ran a marathon."

"It's a workout, getting through the woods on crutches."

"Okay." He seemed less than convinced. "Y'know, if you want company, all you have to do is ask."

She didn't say the answer that ran through her head. No good. It's not safe to be with me right now. They're after me, and I'm not sure why. Better you don't get yourself killed being company.

Tyler was a good kid with a good heart, but he had no battle training. She was happiest having him far away while she fought off the attacks.

"Where's Jacob?" she asked.

"Off somewhere. Like usual."

Overhead, the sky was darkening. Reese looked up and frowned. Clouds were blocking out the open spaces between the pines—clouds and something else.

"Tyler," she said, "get inside."

"What? What's going on?"

"Just get inside," she said, reaching for the wall and getting to her feet. Tyler jumped up but didn't make a move to go in. She went to glare at him and saw a sword in his hand. He held it up.

"What's going on?"

"Would you get inside?"

"No. I'm going to help you."

"Fine," she said through gritted teeth. "But whatever happens, it's not my fault."

Inwardly, she laughed with derision at her own words.

Was anything not her fault?

Gathering out of the clouds overhead was a small, tightly circling flock of birds. They grew in size as she stared up at them.

Multiple demons this time? Or just one, spreading itself thin? They did that sometimes, using birds or insects—anything that would stay together in a tight flock and act as one.

Instead of diving as she expected, the flock tightened its circle and kept spiralling. The clouds were growing darker, plunging the cabin into a premature dusk and then shadows almost as deep as night. Thunder rolled.

"Holy smokes," Tyler said. "I can't see anything."

"Just keep your eyes up there," Reese said. "They'll come from there. Keep your eyes up."

She and Tyler angled themselves so they both stood with the cabin at one shoulder and each other at their backs. Swords ready, eyes up.

Not that eyes were much good in darkness this thick.

"What's going on? Reese?"

"I don't know. Stay focused."

An instant later, light broke through the clouds—and the flock dispersed.

Jacob stood at the edge of the clearing, one eyebrow raised.

"Care to explain this?" he asked.

* * * * *

They sat around the card table in the cabin, Reese's crutches leaning against the wall behind her. "I've been picking them off one by one," she said. "They only come for me."

"And you thought it was better not to tell us because . . ."

Tyler's tone was hostile, but she knew it was only because he cared. She hated the sulkiness in her own reply.

"Because I'm enough trouble by myself." She sighed. "I don't know what the demons want or why they're coming after me now, but until that cloud, they've been easy to spot and easy to dispatch. They've come one at a time, in animal forms—sort of. Grotesque, but not hard to take care of."

She shot Tyler a look. "Tyler, that doesn't apply to you. You don't have enough experience. You see a demon, alert us immediately. Don't try to be a hero on your own."

"You're assuming he can handle himself," Tyler said, pointing to Jacob. "Have you ever seen him fight a demon?"

"He's been in the Oneness a long time. He will have learned."

"Doesn't seem all that smart just to tell me not to fight," Tyler said. "I have to learn sometime."

She sighed and pushed away from the table. "What are you saying?"

"Teach me," he said. "Give me some training. God knows I'm going to need it, hanging out with you two."

"I'm not exactly in coaching form," Reese said, glancing at her crutches.

"I am," Jacob said. "I'll train him."

* * * * *

Renegade   13

Reese watched Jacob and Tyler duel. The older man was hard on the younger, giving him few breaks and little mercy, but he coached as they fought, drawing out the best in him. Tyler had broken into a sweat within minutes and found himself on his back three times in a row. Each time Jacob extended a hand, pulled him back to his feet, and resumed the fight with a few words of instruction.

Reese sat on the front step of the cabin and let her mind rehearse her own battles. Watching Tyler fall made her wince, and question. She was wounded. And alone, or choosing to be. The creatures had come to her in powerful, frightening forms. Yes, she was a good fighter, and yes, she could normally handle a few demons without too much trouble, but it didn't make sense to her—not really—that she was still alive.

Why didn't they come in greater force? Or more strategically, to catch her off guard?

It was almost like they were approaching her this way on purpose. Like—

Jacob drove Tyler up against a pile of rocks, and he tripped and sprawled backwards, yelling this time. That had to hurt.

Barely sweating, Jacob extended his hand again. Tyler stayed on the ground, panting, not reaching for the outstretched hand. He shook his head, too out of breath to say anything.

"If this was a real fight, you'd have lost right here," Jacob said. "Never lose track of your surroundings. You do, and any obstacle becomes a trap."

Tyler nodded and struggled into a sitting position. He mopped his forehead, streaking it with dirt and blood from a scratch. "Can we take a break?" he asked.

Jacob looked disgusted, but he let his sword dissolve from his hand. "Fine."

Tyler kept his own sword balanced across his knees. "Whaddya think?" he asked Reese. "Did I learn anything?"

"I hope so," she said, putting her own thoughts aside for a minute. "I can work with you too, if you want."

Tyler nodded in Jacob's direction. "Not necessary. You can't possibly school me worse than him."

His face grew more serious. "You think we're going to get a bigger attack?"

"Maybe," Reese said. "Maybe the others have been scouts. Either way, we're not going to be here for them to find."

She shot Jacob a look at that statement. It had been his idea to hole up here, and he'd been resistant to any suggestion that they should leave.

"We'll go," he said, nodding. "Soon. Maybe tomorrow."

"Not now? Tonight?"

"I'm not ready to leave yet."

"This isn't just about you," Tyler shot out. "Reese could be in trouble."

"I doubt leaving here will actually get her out of that trouble. And I don't want to stay here just for my own sake. I'm doing what I do for you—both of you."

Tyler rolled his eyes and looked questioningly at Reese. She didn't answer. She didn't know what Jacob was waiting for and didn't want to press him for an answer. His answers to the questions she did ask were challenging enough.

* * * * *

He offered another of those answers that night as she sat in the darkness, losing herself in the pine shadows with only the bright pinpricks of stars high above to offset them. The inside of the cabin felt too constricting; she wanted air. And to watch for trouble.

Her hands were empty; the sword didn't materialize. She assumed the woods were likewise bare. For the moment.

She didn't welcome his presence as he came out and sat down beside her, but he didn't seem to care.

"These may not be attacks," he said abruptly.

"What are you talking about?"

"The demons. They may not be attacking you."

"They do attack me."

"Because you're meeting them with your sword drawn. You're confronting them as for battle—provoking them. They have no choice."

She shook her head. "Sometimes you talk like a crazy man."

"Has there been anything different about these entities? Anything . . . unusual?"

"You're talking about demons."

"Even the demonic has its own normal. You've encountered enough to know what is and what isn't."

"Yes," she said finally. "They've been . . . like animals, but not . . . not like they usually are."

"Describe them."

"They're a pastiche. The last one, it was a wolf. But a spider too. I've never seen a demon in a form like that."

He nodded. "It makes sense. They're coming to you like this for a reason, Reese. And it isn't to fight you."

Her eyes flashed as she turned to face him. She could barely make out his features in the darkness; the cabin was dark on the inside too, with no light escaping from cracks in the door. "What are you trying to say?"

"Demons that embody like you say these are doing are not working for anyone. They're taking on forms as they please, trying to establish an identity or personality. They don't do that if they have a master, because they simply allow the master's personality and identity to inform theirs."

She raised an eyebrow. "I'm being approached by demonic mutts?"

"They see a master in you," Jacob said. "They're offering their help."

She was on her feet before she knew what she was doing. Shaking.

"Don't just reject this gift, Reese," Jacob said, his voice rising. "They've never come to me like this. They're offering themselves to you because you're a warrior and a power they can recognize. Most of us have to earn their allegiance. You already have."

She turned on him. "I don't want that! I don't want anything to do with them!"

"Don't you?" he asked. "What if they can help you get what you really want?"

"And what is that?" Reese asked, trembling even harder now. The sword was beginning to form in her hand, but it was only half-there, a response to her anxiety.

"The same thing I want," Jacob said. "Justice."

He stood. She heard the boards creaking under his weight. He paused at the cabin door and turned back to her.

"They didn't trust you to deal with him," Jacob said. "They were afraid you would demand justice if he didn't change. So if he doesn't—if he hasn't—they will simply let him go on, unchanged and unrepentant, and gloating over the damage he's done you. Think about that."

He went through the door and shut it behind him.

And Reese still shook.

"Stay close to me," *she had whispered.*

Patrick and Tony crouched behind her, both with swords drawn, both wearing dark clothes and grim expressions with an undercurrent of excitement, even joy. Their cell had been defending against the hive with no real success for months. And now Reese had brought them to its source.

Garish light did little to illuminate the parking lot, casting deep shadows instead. Reese had chosen an old Buick to hunker down behind. Its tires were a little flat, and grass was pushing through the pavement beneath it. The warehouse loomed beyond, lit by perimeter lights that attracted insects and hummed with an electric buzz. Men were unloading a truck at one of the docks; Reese and company were waiting for them to leave.

This was it. The core, the locus of demonic activity and presence that had been fuelling the hive. She had found it, after months of tracking, and she knew that now was the time to strike. They did not expect an attack. And the Spirit was leading—she knew tonight was the time.

The cell was not entirely behind her. David had tried to talk her out of an attack, saying it was too dangerous and they didn't really know enough about the core to strike it with so little preparation. But she knew what the Spirit was saying, and Patrick and Tony felt it too . . . enough, at least, to trust her to lead them here. And anyway, wasn't this what they had spent their entire lives preparing for? Every attack, every skirmish, every fight with the demons had been preparation for a bigger battle, one that would strike a real blow, make a real difference. She'd felt that in her gut since she was a girl. David would see. He would understand and admit that he'd been wrong.

Reese crouched in the shadows and soaked up that assurance, the strength of Oneness. She felt her companions' spirits bonded with hers, and beyond them the cell—even David—giving her strength like marrow in her bones. She drew on every one of them as she waited and steeled herself for the fight: on their presence, their power, their unity, their love.

Oneness was the truest, the most real thing in Reese's life. She was strong, a warrior with few equals in a cell full of fighters, because of the strength of her belief in their bond and all that it meant. And now, in this moment, Oneness and Spirit throbbed through her veins like a hot pulse, bringing her body and spirit to life.

The men finished unloading and turned their attention to the back of their truck, leaving the loading door ajar.

"Now," Reese said, and all three moved at once, as if they'd known this opportunity would come exactly when it did. They ran silently through the shadows and slipped through the door before anyone knew they were there. The interior was almost entirely dark, lit only by traces of the lights outside, and those winked out as the dock door closed with a rattle of chains and tin and the truck departed.

For a moment they stood alone in the darkness, back to back, forming a tight circle. Dust, diesel, and electricity tinged the air.

They were the meeting place of three worlds—physical and spiritual, and the Oneness, straddling the other two. The spiritual world had not yet noticed their presence. It would only take a moment. Reese could feel the presence of the demons, unbodied but there on the other side of the visible.

So, while hers was still the element of surprise, with the rush of Spirit still pumping through her veins, she began the attack with a single word: "Now."

Patrick and Tony raised their swords and let out a war cry. All three surged forward into a battle with creatures that barely had time to materialize, their swords made of spirit and effective even against the invisible. The demonic came together as wisps of white and grey cloud around them, dispersed and dispatched before they could offer any real resistance.

How many there were, she never really knew. The air felt thick with them, thicker than she had ever felt it. If she were alone, she knew she would stand no chance. But she was not alone. The men with her were among the best fighters in the cell—in the country, really. She herself was one of the best in the nation. They empowered each other as only Oneness could do. And the Spirit—

She had never felt the Spirit so strongly.

She felt as though she was carrying the energy of the world-wide millions of Oneness with her.

As they fought, she could feel the sins of the demonic dispersing with them. She could feel the lies, the wounds, the suicidal thoughts and insanity. She could feel the abuse and the substance addictions, the temptations, the domination, the witchcraft. Everything they had been working in the city, through the hive and otherwise. Everything they represented, going to pieces along with them.

Though it was dark in the warehouse, light wasn't needed. They were fighting blind with a sight that saw what the eyes could not. She had never operated so purely in the spiritual world, never come so close to leaving the physical behind.

The fight was a blur in her memory. More a rapid series of sensations than a linear story. One thing only she remembered with clarity: she remembered the moment Patrick died. The demons had begun to pull themselves together into more discrete, visual forms, forcing the Oneness back into a more physical way of fighting that was, to her surprise, harder. Relying on their eyes seemed to rob them of ability to respond to invisible cues. At the same time, there were far fewer of the creatures—it seemed the attack had already been successful. They had decimated the core.

Reese had spun around to face an attack from a winged thing flying straight at her, and when she had driven her sword through its heart and watched it fly apart into wisps of smoke, she heard a cry of anguish and turned to see Patrick fall to his knees. The demon behind him, formed in the shape of a tall man, raised its battle axe to deal a death blow. Reese threw her sword like a spear and pierced the demon through the heart.

She rushed to Patrick, but it was too late. Her sword disintegrated beyond her as she grabbed Patrick's hand and held it tight, and he clung to hers—a grip too strong for a dying man. His face was streaked with sweat and dust, but he smiled.

"We did it."

She wanted to believe he would live. She knew better. Their connection was strong—strong from a cell life together, strong from a shared passion, strong from a last battle fought side by side. She could feel life ebbing from him and knew that his spirit was about to fly.

There was some hope, some excitement in that. But the grief quickly overtaking her drowned out her sense of it. It didn't seem fair—that she should go home and celebrate victory while Patrick would never leave the warehouse in bodily form. That she would be welcomed back to the home they both loved, wrapped in its warmth, while he went on to a strange, foreign journey.

Anger at the demonic and all that fed it rose within her.

"I'll avenge you," she choked out. "I'll see to it that the hive is finished forever—that the demonic never forgets you."

He tried to smile again, but his body was in the throes of letting go—and he was gone.

* * * * *

Reese and Tony returned to the cell house in their run-down city neighbourhood in the wee hours of the morning, exhausted, sore, grieving, and victorious.

Angelica, Tony's twin, was the first out the door as they walked up the cracked cement to the house. She grabbed him, half a hug, half a demand. "Where have you been?"

"Beating the hive," Tony said.

Angelica's eyes raked them both, filling with tears. "Where's Patrick?"

"He's gone on," Reese said, steeling her voice.

Angelica let out a sob and ran back to the door, disappearing inside.

It wasn't quite the welcome Reese had expected. Not that Angelica's grief was a surprise, but there was something else— something almost ominous in the short, fearful way she had spoken. And in the way no one else emerged from the house, though the lights were all on and it was clear the cell was waiting for them.

Tony reached out and squeezed her arm just before they stepped through the front door.

Inside, the cell was gathered in the common room, faces grim.

David, especially, was grim.

And worse. Accusing.

"Reese, where is Patrick?" he said.

"He fell," she said. "I'm sorry. But David—we brought down the core. They've been destroyed. The Spirit—"

"Reese, you need to be silent." His voice was shaking as though it hurt him to speak, as though he didn't want to say any of this. As though all he wanted was for everything to be all right. But that reluctance only added to the way his words slapped her across the face. It gave his words authority.

She obeyed.

"I told you not to go," he said.

"I . . ." She swallowed and looked around, trying to find a friend. The faces of the cell members, her brothers and sisters—the marrow in her bones—were blank. Frozen. Eyes lowered, refusing to meet hers. "I had to follow the Spirit."

"You've insisted for weeks on following your own ways, your own will, and calling it the Spirit. You've acted against the Oneness."

"I only . . ."

"Reese, a man is dead. One of ours is dead. Patrick is dead." His face twisted with grief. "Isn't that enough to tell you how wrong you've been? How deceived?"

Silence.

He went on. "I've tried to help you see reason, to show you the truth. You've resisted every step of the way. Resisted to the point of killing your own brother—he would not be dead without you, Reese."

His words were so impossibly awful as to be nonsensical. She heard them; they sent the room—the world—spinning. But she couldn't comprehend.

"You have to be cut off."

He was still talking . . . she couldn't follow.

"You're a danger to the Oneness . . . to the cell and to all of us . . ."

And the words she could not forget.

"You have to be exiled . . ."

* * * * *

"There's one part of that night you aren't remembering," came Jacob's voice from the darkness behind her. She jumped and turned, but she couldn't see him. How many hours had she been pacing in the dark under the pines, replaying her memories? The cabin was not far away, but it was plunged in shadow.

"Every member of the Oneness has a special gift," Jacob said. "Mine is sight. And I've seen your memories—you're missing something. Something you need to know if you're ever going to find peace."

"What is it?" She didn't want to ask the words. Didn't want to give Jacob this much access to her heart. But they came out her mouth anyway.

"Ask someone who was there," he said.

The piece of the woods where she was lit up—

It wasn't Jacob she was talking to.

It was a creature standing on two legs like a man and speaking with Jacob's voice, but it was covered with black fur—a bear perhaps.

"Demon," she said, threateningly, and her sword formed in her hand.

Late.

It simply repeated the words, "Ask someone who was there."

Her hand was shaking. She didn't raise the sword in aggression. "You?"

"Will you allow me to show you?"

It was still Jacob's voice, unnerving in its familiarity as it came from the mouth of something so decidedly inhuman.

She knew what she ought to say.

That she ought to refuse any communion with this creature—this enemy of all that she was.

But she said, "Yes."

It stretched out its hands, and somehow it was closer now—standing right before her. Its massive, clawed bear hands surrounded her head, and she was back there, in the warehouse, standing in a swirl of cloud and smoke and unearthly light. She was locked in hand-to-hand battle, but this time she turned away from her enemy, leaving it undealt with, and faced Patrick instead.

In doing so, she saw what she had never seen before.

That moments before Patrick was stabbed in the back, his attention had been pulled away from the battle by someone standing on the high catwalk that rimmed the warehouse.

Someone human.

And as Reese looked, the human figure was illuminated, and she saw him clearly. She was aware that out of her line of sight, Patrick had been stabbed and fallen.

She saw the man on the catwalk respond with satisfaction.

The vision dissipated, and Reese stood in the clearing of the woods with tears streaming down her face.

She knew the man on the catwalk. They all did.

David had been there.

The creature—the demon, she reminded herself—was still standing in the clearing with her, in the preternatural light. Waiting.

"Why did you show me that?" she asked.

It began to answer.

She did not want to hear.

She screamed and threw her sword straight through its heart. The creature let out a tortuous bellow and crumpled, its human features fading away and its height shrinking as the body turned back to that of a black bear.

"No, no, no, no," she said, her protests dwindling to a whisper.

She had nearly allowed a demon to bring her into its confidence.

And now she felt what she had never, ever felt after a fight before—remorse. For killing one of the demonic.

She heard shouts, and a light—natural this time, flicked on inside the cabin, followed by the porch light and then the sweeping and bobbing beacon of a flashlight. "Reese! Reese, where are you? What's going on?"

Tyler arrived in the clearing, rubbing sleep out of his eyes. "What's happening? Are you okay?" His light flashed onto the bear carcass, and he stepped back involuntarily. "What . . . did you kill that?"

Jacob was just behind him, far less shaken and holding a

stronger flashlight. He shone it on the bear for a full three minutes without speaking.

The other two quieted, waiting for him.

"Well," he said, grimly, "if that was what I think it was, our wait here is over. Reese? Do you have something to tell us?"

She shook her head.

She couldn't tell them. Couldn't speak.

They left the cabin in the morning. Jacob didn't explain, just said it was time to go. Tyler seemed happy to be leaving, and Reese was more than ready to leave the clearing behind. Their first stop would be a logging town on the way out of the mountains, where they could access a laundromat, groceries, and a pay phone.

The latter was for Reese. It was about time she put in a call to Lieutenant Jackson and explained why she wasn't bringing his prisoner back.

Whether she ever would depended on what side she was on, and she wasn't sure about that yet.

But Jackson had been helpful, and had trusted her, so she called. If she hadn't, she might never have gotten the message.

"One of our witnesses has been trying pretty desperately to reach you," Jackson told her. She could guess who, but she asked anyway. Yes, it was Julie.

She got the number for the safe house and called.

"Reese," Julie told her, "there's something Jacob needs to know. Some of your cell came here yesterday and told us that Clint has been defeated—they stripped him of his powers somehow. But Reese, Clint isn't his real name. Or even his real face. He's been disguising himself."

Reese frowned. "So his real name is . . ."

"Franz Bertoller."

Reese's blood ran cold at the name. It called up Jacob's story all over again—his terrible, world-altering story of loss and the miscarriage of justice. Franz Bertoller was a monster. The man responsible for the death of Jacob's wife, for Jacob's descent into torment and conversion to a new vision of the Oneness, for the bombing of the old Oneness cell twenty years ago that had affected so many in Reese's own life, for the suffering of countless people.

Jacob had long believed him to be dead of old age. Reese had seen the man's gravestone.

"He's alive?"

"Yes."

"Isn't he . . ."

"He's an old man. Very old. Don't ask me what keeps him alive."

"You're right," Reese said. "Jacob does need to know this."

"Richard said they can't charge him with Clint's crimes because he lost his disguise when he lost his powers, and the police can't connect Bertoller with Clint. Especially considering that as far as they're concerned, Bertoller's dead."

"Right."

"There's something else. Something I thought you should know."

She knew it before Julie said it. "They brought David back?"

"Yes. No change of heart. He's back in jail, waiting for charges."

Reese's heart wrestled with itself—she didn't know if she felt broken or elated by the news. "Oh."

"Richard said the hive is destroyed anyway."

"Oh," she said again. It was good news.

She had chased the hive for years. Had nearly destroyed it herself before the exile. She should feel triumphant, victorious.

She didn't.

Whatever had happened in the last battle, she hadn't been part of it. She'd been off with Jacob, trying to convert him and instead finding all of her own most cherished beliefs put on trial.

And the verdict was not yet in.

But Bertoller . . .

She did have to tell him. He had to know.

"Thank you, Julie."

Julie's voice was kind. "I'm sorry if this news isn't the easiest to take. About David."

Alarm struck her at the words. "What do you mean? It's great news that the hive is finished."

"That's not what I meant. I meant I'm sorry that David didn't change his heart."

"Oh. Yes."

Reese hung up after saying good-bye, wooden and hating her own conflicted feelings. She should be sorry David hadn't changed. The village cell had determined to do all they could to help him, redeem him. She should be heartbroken that he had refused their help. Wasn't he her brother? Didn't she want him saved?

But she just kept seeing the image of him standing on the catwalk in the warehouse, watching Patrick die with satisfaction. And then pinning his death on her.

Exiling her.

And behind that, all the years she had trusted him, considered him a brother, even loved him.

She exited the phone booth she'd used to make the calls and nodded to Tyler, who was leaning against a lamppost just beside it. She didn't even know the name of the town where they were—just that it was in the mountains, inland and north of nowhere, with foothills and a desert between them and the coast.

She forced her thoughts back to the original call. "The lieutenant says he trusts us."

"I hope that's a good idea."

She shot Tyler a glare.

"Hey, Reese, easy. You know as well as I do that we don't know what we're doing. Just following Jacob around and hoping he has some kind of good plan."

She leaned on one of her crutches and used her free hand to wipe sweat from her forehead. "It's hot as blazes again." The air smelled like burnt pine. Everything out here was dry.

"I miss the water. The bay," Tyler said.

"Well, maybe we can get back there soon."

Tyler was quiet, falling into step beside Reese as she hobbled down the street toward the public parking lot ringed with pines where they'd left the car and Jacob. Crutch, hop. Crutch, hop.

"I'll stay with you as long as you need," he said finally. "The water can wait."

She turned and regarded him, his long, curly hair making his face boyish despite several days' worth of blond stubble on his chin and cheeks.

"Thanks, Tyler."

"You deserve to have someone stick by you."

"You don't really believe in what I'm doing, do you?"

"Sure I do. You need to figure out where you stand on some issues. That's important. I believe in that."

"But you don't like where I'm going on those issues."

"Jacob scares me," Tyler said. "I don't love it when you entertain his questions. But I can't stop you. And somebody has to ask the hard stuff. I'm just along for the ride."

"You're a good friend."

He shrugged and smiled. The smile faded quickly. "So what else did you find out?"

"Nothing much."

"No answers to why you're being attacked?"

"No."

Tyler stopped. "You learned something. Spill."

She tried to act affronted. "What?"

"I didn't think you could get more uneasy, but you're worse since you stepped out of that phone booth. You're not like this because Lieutenant Jackson trusts us."

Reese sighed. The boy was perceptive.

"I talked to Julie. She said David's back."

Tyler brightened. "What? They're done? The battle is over?"

"Seems that way. Apparently Richard visited her and told her that the hive is finished. But David didn't change his heart. They brought him back to jail and he'll face charges."

He slowed down and scanned her face—she could feel his eyes on her even though she didn't look at him. "Are you happy about that?"

"I don't know what I feel about that," she confessed. "I want justice to be done. It's good that he'll face trial."

But he won't face vengeance, she thought. And I promised Patrick vengeance. Justice—against the real enemy.

They crossed the street, thumping across the blazing pavement to the nondescript parking lot. Pines surrounded it on three sides; on the fourth was the back of a one-story commercial building with its paint peeling.

"Are you happy that he didn't change?"

"Tyler . . ."

"I just think you should talk about it."

She sighed and shook her head. "I don't know. Do you have to ask questions like that?"

"You do. You're asking yourself. I just think you shouldn't handle them alone."

She smiled and chuckled. "You really believe in the Oneness."

"Of course I do."

"It's just impressive. For someone so new."

"Didn't you believe like this when you were new?"

She didn't want to even think about that. She had believed more than anyone she knew. Reese had always been the blazing idealist, the one set on fire by her own passionate convictions. She'd believed with everything in her that the Oneness was life—that "never alone" was the only watchword she needed. She'd let the Oneness and its goals define her and had poured her whole life into its service. Until David exiled her.

Somehow, even though that had been a lie, it had changed everything for her.

Maybe that was why she felt it necessary to entertain Jacob's questions. Maybe, by following new ways of thinking about the Oneness, she could rediscover belief. Start over somehow. Rediscover the love that had changed her life once.

"I just can't quite come back yet," she whispered. "I'll get there, Tyler. I just need time."

He nodded, but he looked unhappy.

They crossed the parking lot to the car. They had left Jacob waiting for them, but he wasn't there—no big surprise. The man was anything but patient and docile. Patience and docility, in fact, were two of the Oneness qualities that he generally abhorred.

"So now what?" Tyler asked.

Reese reached for the door handle, pulling her hand back as the metal threatened to burn her fingers. "Ouch. Now we . . . Oh, there he is."

Tyler looked over the top of the car. Jacob was striding across the parking lot like he owned it—like he owned the whole town. Dressed in his work pants and button-up shirt, with a dark beard covering most of his face, he looked incredibly uncomfortable in the heat. What they could see of his face was flushed beet red.

Reese tossed her crutches into the backseat and hopped into the driver's side as usual. Thankfully it was her left ankle that was broken, and she could stretch it out best when she was driving. Jacob sat beside her, mopping his face with a handkerchief. The inside of the station wagon felt like a blast furnace. She turned it on and felt hot air blow out the vents. The air conditioning worked, but only intermittently—and even when it was running, "worked" was a slight overstatement.

Tyler eased himself into the backseat and didn't say a word.

Jacob started to say something about the heat in towns and how reflective it was of man's need to turn everything into concrete. Reese wasn't really listening.

One phrase was pounding through her head, made more hellish by the hot air:

Franz Bertoller is alive.

The man Jacob had failed to execute so many years ago.

The man whose crimes had prompted him to rethink the entire way the Oneness operated, to conclude that they had compromised and lost their power and integrity by failing to bring such evil to justice. The man who had destroyed much of the Oneness twenty years ago, including Jacob's beloved first wife and Mary's twin brother and even Chris's father, though he wasn't Oneness but was only connected to them . . .

And not only was he alive, but he had been operating as Clint. Jacob's one-time right-hand man.

"The plot thickens," she muttered under her breath.

"What did you say?" Jacob asked.

"I said it's really hot."

Liar, her thoughts said. Why don't you just tell him?

She would. She just wasn't sure how yet.

When they sprang Jacob out of jail, where he was awaiting charges of manslaughter at least, and possibly murder, after the death of a man who had been in the care of his community, it had been on the agreement of a week spent examining one another's case. Jacob would try to convince Reese that he was right about his cause, and then she would try to convince him that he was wrong.

So far they had stretched the agreement past a week, and all she had accomplished was discovering that she wasn't convinced of her own side.

So now it was her turn, her game, and she was on a mission not so much to convince Jacob as to convince herself.

That, or give up and change sides.

Once upon a time she would not have thought that was possible, but a lot of things had changed.

Jacob went back to complaining about the heat and man-made misery. She wondered if he ever encountered a subject he wasn't passionate about, but she doubted it. The strength of the man's spirit was gravitational enough to pull planets out of orbit.

By contrast, she felt about as powerful and influential as a flea trying to change the direction of a dog. She might irritate, but she couldn't do much to change the course of anything.

She knew the case she should be making. That the task of the Oneness was to hold the world, even the universe, together by counteracting the destructive forces of darkness, and that they did so through love, service, and compassionate reaching out to ordinary humans while battling the demonic wherever they found it.

Somehow, with the image of David's face in the warehouse haunting her, the case felt weak.

"Perhaps you should consider," Jacob boomed out of nowhere, as though he was reading her thoughts—which maybe he was—"the role of justice in any love worth the name."

She didn't answer, pretending that driving was taking too much of her concentration. Despite the fact that they were in a two-stoplight town in the middle of nowhere and that traffic was nearly nonexistent at this time of day.

"It's Reese's turn," Tyler piped up from the backseat.

Jacob likewise ignored him.

Aren't we a happy crew, Reese thought, turning out of the town and toward the narrow highway that headed back into the woods and toward the cabin.

Franz Bertoller is alive.

That thought came pounding back through, insisting that

she not ignore it.

She had agreed with Julie that Jacob needed to know.

But it was going to change things if he did.

For both of them.

She gave the car more gas, pushing it forward like she could drive away from the course-altering power of Julie's news.

She couldn't.

Without signalling, she slowed down and pulled to the side of the road. Gravel and pine needles crunched under their tires, and the car listed to the right toward the ditch beside them.

She threw it into park and sat back. "Franz Bertoller is alive," she said.

About as subtle as an atomic bomb.

Jacob went white.

The car was silent.

After a moment he said, "That's impossible."

"It's not. He must have faked his death. He was demon-possessed. He's been . . ." She almost choked. She cleared her throat and kept going. "He's been going under a different face. Clint. Clint is Franz Bertoller."

Silence.

She kept on, not sure what reaction she had been expecting but wishing Jacob would do or say something. "The cell figured it out. They've stripped him of his power somehow, but he's reverted to his old form and they can't pin Clint's crimes to him, so . . ."

Jacob pounded his fist into the dashboard so hard that Reese thought he was going to go through it, and then he swore, jerked the car door open, and stalked up the winding road, visibly trembling.

"Wow," Tyler said.

She wasn't sure if he was commenting on her news or on Jacob's reaction, but she said, "I know."

Apparently the news didn't take Jacob long to process. "You will help me go after him," he said when he got back in the car.

She didn't know if it was a question.

But the answer was yes.

She would.

It was as good a way as any to find answers, and somehow, she knew she couldn't leave him to do this alone.

"Reese . . ." Tyler said in the backseat, but they both ignored him.

"What do you want to do?" she asked.

"Find him. Bring him to justice."

"What about . . ."

Jacob's face was anguished. "I'm dismayed at the news that he was disguising himself as Clint. That he was operating right under my nose. It shows blindness on my part. I'm an honest man, I'll admit this right now: to the extent you said I should not have been working with him, you were right. I was deceived in trusting him, clearly. The fruit of that is in the death of that trucker and the trouble my whole community is in. I take responsibility for that."

"I—"

He didn't wait for her full response. "But deception is one thing. Evil is another. This man is evil. If he is not brought to justice, he will do far more damage. We can't let him, Reese. We have to find out where he is and go after him. I have to finish what I started all those years ago."

And somehow, it was that last line that brought her fully on board. She knew better than to embrace personal vendettas. She knew that the Oneness was a body, a community, not a collective of renegades on their own personal courses. But she understood.

"Yes, I'll help," she said.

In the back, Tyler sat against the seat with a thump.

"You don't have to come," she said.

"Of course I'm coming."

"You have to be on our side," Jacob said.

"I'm on your side. You two are my family. That's my side."

"On the side of our cause."

"I will come with you," Tyler said. "That's all I'm saying."

"That's good enough," Reese said.

"Very well." Jacob's eyes, fixed until now on Reese's face, flicked to the backseat and rested on Tyler for a second before returning to Reese. "What do you know about where he is?"

"Nothing. Julie didn't know."

He looked surprised. "Julie?"

"Richard visited her and told her. She called the prison, and they put me in touch with her."

His face clouded. "I failed her. I failed all of them. Bringing that . . ."

"You didn't know," Reese said, softly. "We can all be deceived."

Tyler made a noise, but she continued to ignore him.

"So who would know?" Jacob asked.

"Richard might. He's the one who told Julie everything."

Besides passing on Julie's message, Lieutenant Jackson had also told her that the village cell had been trying to reach her. She hadn't called them back. She couldn't, not yet. She missed them, but she had to finish her job before she went home.

If she still had a home at the end of it.

So she told him, "I don't think we can go to Richard. The cell would try to stop y—us."

"Would Clint—Bertoller—have contacted any of his cohorts?"

"You can't go back to any prison," Reese pointed out. "They might not let you walk out again. I don't know how Lieutenant Jackson is covering for us as it is."

He was quiet, pondering for a moment. Then, "You're right. It would be foolish to jeopardize our freedom."

Your freedom, Reese thought, but she didn't say that.

"We could reach some of his other cohorts."

That took her a moment. Sitting in the car under the shade of pines that did little to negate the heat of the sun, with the barren road winding off ahead of them in silence, the suggestion felt incongruous. When she figured out what he meant, it punched her in the gut.

"You're not going to keep trying to work with the demons."

"I told you. Demons are just power. They're only servants of evil because evil people harness them."

Her fingers tightened around the steering wheel. "Right . . . and that's why they're trying to kill me."

"I've already told you what I think about that. Unless I miss my guess, they proved my point in the clearing last night—in the encounter you haven't told us anything about."

Reese didn't say a word.

"You'd be better off learning to control them yourself, rather than just fighting them all the time."

"No. And I can't work with you if you try to do that."

He looked out the window, his presence a storm. "Then maybe you'd better let me go alone."

"There has to be another way to find him."

Tyler muttered something in the back.

Another minute passed.

"There is another way," Jacob said. "But you will regret it if we take it."

"Try me."

"We can wait for him to strike. He needs to get power back, if you're right that they stripped him of it. He'll build it the same way he always has—through sacrifice. By destroying others. And then we can hope he leaves us a trail we can follow." He turned and glared at her. "But you will have to take responsibility for letting him strike when you could have used other powers to find him first."

Tyler said his piece again, louder this time so they could both hear him. "Two wrongs don't make a right."

"You go ahead and believe that," Jacob said. "I'll let you lead on this only because you need to truly understand the gravity of your compromise. You need to understand what the Oneness's refusal to use real power is costing this world."

"Fine," Reese said, her voice shaking. "I'll accept that. I've been fighting demons most of my life; I can't suddenly start allying with them."

He shook his head. "You don't understand. But I know— sometimes it takes something life-changing to open your eyes."

As though she hadn't already experienced plenty of that.

Whether or not her eyes had been opened—that, she still couldn't say.

"So what do we do now?" she asked.

"We head for Lincoln. It's where he last operated. Your friends might be foolish enough to let Bertoller go—alive!—but I'll not be foolish enough to keep my distance. I want to be there when he strikes, before he can gain the power he needs."

Richard hung up the phone slowly and shook his head.

"No good?" Mary asked.

"She called," he said. "Jackson said she called. So she got our messages. She'll call us if she wants to."

"What do you think she's doing?" Mary asked.

"I wish I knew."

Seated at the kitchen table, Diane looked up from a newspaper. "Figuring things out, I'd guess. Her life hasn't been exactly simple recently, and you sent her off to talk to the devil himself, from what Chris said."

"Jacob is a brother."

"One with a tongue like a fox."

Richard sighed. "I think she'll be all right. She just needs some time, and some space—clearly."

The sound of children's laughter outside turned his head.

Nick was dousing Alicia with a garden hose, and she was shrieking and telling him to stop it. Both of them were laughing their heads off.

"We can't do anything about Reese right now," Richard said. "Nothing except trust her. She's got Tyler with her, and they've both got good heads and better hearts. I'm not worried. I do wish we could do something about Jacob, but I think we'd better trust Reese with that too."

"It's not that I don't trust her," Mary said. "It's just that I'm worried about what might have happened. If Jacob got the jump on her somehow."

"She called Lieutenant Jackson, and he said she sounded just fine. Just collecting her messages and letting him know she wouldn't be back for a little while. I think she's okay."

Jacob was the last loose end, the one part of the hive they had not managed to get hold of—all because Reese had defaulted her post in some sense, but Richard refused to think of it that way. He would trust her. She had earned it.

"I want to go back to Lincoln, though, and see Julie again," he said. "She and her daughter could use the solidarity of the Oneness right now, and I think Reese would want us to take care of them."

He looked up when Melissa walked into the kitchen, smiling faintly as she looked out at the loud water fight outside the window.

"Looks like fun," she said.

April trailed in after her, dressed for a run. "Nick hasn't had fun like that maybe ever. I'm glad you brought Alicia."

Mary raised her eyebrows. "You're going for a run in this heat?"

April shrugged and pulled her blonde hair into a ponytail. "I have to get my strength back sometime."

"Heat exhaustion doesn't seem like the best way."

"It's cooler down by the water."

She was out the door before Mary could respond. Mary just laughed and shook her head, laughing even more when Nick turned the hose fully on April as she jogged past.

"It's a growing family we've got," she told Richard.

"Who would have seen that coming?" he asked. Alicia had become Oneness while she was still hiding out with Melissa in the cave on Tempter's Mountain, just suddenly opening herself to the Spirit. Nick had yet to become One, but it was only a matter of time. It was common for children who lived in cells to act as functional members of the Oneness before they were actually Joined.

Alicia's brother, Jordan, had disappeared. Richard and Tony had spent two days searching for him on the mountain, to no avail.

"You did all you could," Mary said softly.

"Sometimes," Richard answered, "that is a terrible limit."

"That's why it isn't just you," she said. "That's why we have the Oneness."

He nodded and looked away from the window. Outside, April had abandoned her run, wrestled the hose away from Nick, and was now soaking both children. Melissa had glued herself to the window and was watching, deep in thought. Richard glanced her way but found he couldn't keep watching her. He hadn't known how hard it would be for him to have her here—because once again, "all you can do" was a terrible limit. He could do nothing to save her life, and he hated that.

All he could do, all the village cell could do, was act as a hospice and help her die in peace and surrounded by family.

She turned away and seated herself at the table across from Diane, pouring herself a glass of cold lemonade. Every movement was graceful, long, slender fingers somehow calling attention to themselves even when they weren't making music.

Mary laid a hand on Richard's shoulder and left it there, imparting all the sympathy and strength she could.

He covered her hand with his and squeezed her fingers without a word.

"So," she said, "you'll go into town to see Julie. You want company?"

"I don't see why not." He motioned toward the pair who had regained control of the hose and were now soaking April from head to foot. "We might as well take those two along. They can play with Miranda."

"She's a good bit older, isn't she?"

"She is, but . . ." He hesitated. "She isn't mature. I don't think it benefited Jacob's goals to raise mature people. Or else his control just didn't give them room, even if he intended it that way. I noticed it in some of the others too—it's like they're years younger than they should be."

"Childlikeness can be a good thing," Mary said, raising an

eyebrow as April shrieked and chased an equally shrieking Nick around in a circle.

"Childlikeness, yes. Childishness, no. Jacob kept them childish—underequipped and underempowered. Dangerous in a war."

Mary shook her head. "I wish—"

"We all do."

Neither said Reese's name again. There was no point in talking about it. There was nothing they could do.

* * * * *

As Jacob drove, Reese closed her eyes and conjured up images from years of battles, years of hunting down demons, years of thinking she was making a real difference in the world. On the surface, she was. They had broken the backs of a few criminals, but there was always another to take its place. They had freed a few people from torment, but there was no guarantee they hadn't walked right back into it, or into torment of another kind. The Oneness supposedly held the world together, but the forces of entropy were so powerful it was hard to see it as anything but a losing battle.

She wondered what would happen if they stopped. If they just gave up. If people would destroy themselves, sending the earth up in an atomic supernova, or if the laws of physics would actually unravel and cease holding the universe in place.

For a moment it struck her as absurd that they saw themselves as having so much impact. Were they just deluded?

Had she just been lied to?

She shook her head. Even Jacob didn't believe that; he just believed the Oneness was going about its work the wrong way, that they needed to wrest greater power into their hands and go after the human agents of evil and deterioration to restore the balance of justice in the world. But it was funny how asking those questions could open the door to more.

Not only to questions, really, but to doubt.

She had never been a doubter.

She didn't think she liked the label.

Her ankle was throbbing, and she gingerly shifted position and then closed her eyes again. At the moment she didn't even want to look at where they might be going.

"I bought something while we were in town," Jacob said out of nowhere. He inclined his head toward a satchel on the floor, a bag he had been hauling around with him since they got him out of the corrective facility. He obviously wanted Reese to pick it up, so gingerly, she did.

"Open it up," he said.

With a suspicious look at him, she slowly opened the bag. Inside, a thick plastic bag was wrapped around a purchase. She unwrapped it, feeling its heavy weight, and found herself looking at three good-sized hunting knives.

She cast an easy glance over her shoulder at Tyler, who was sitting forward to see. He was frowning.

"What are these for?" he asked.

"Even before you told me about Bertoller, I knew this journey might take us into violent waters," Jacob said. "Better not to be unarmed."

"We have our Spirit swords," Tyler said.

"And those only work against spiritual enemies."

Tyler folded his arms. "All our enemies are spiritual."

"We're still proving that, aren't we?" Jacob asked.

Reese had put two of the knives down and held just one now, pulling it out of its sheath and brandishing it carefully. It felt strange—its physicality a mirror of the Spirit sword she knew so well, its solid presence in her hand at once like and completely unlike the hilt that had formed there so many times. Just as the enemy it was meant for was like and completely unlike the enemies she had fought for years. An unexpected memory struck her: Patrick talking about how much he liked hunting and how it had made him better in battle. He liked knives, bows, and arrows, not guns. She had told him she preferred bloodless targets.

That was all before he died.

She smiled faintly at Tyler, who was watching her with obvious worry. "Patrick would have liked these," she said. "He was a hunter."

Tyler had seen and talked with Patrick several times—Reese's old friend had come to him as part of the cloud even before Tyler was Joined. "I don't think he would have liked what you're thinking of doing with them," he said.

"Your problem," Jacob boomed, "is that you lack purpose, boy. You think the Oneness is all about your—that it's about having friends, having community. You don't yet understand that you are here for a reason, and that reason is combating the powers of destruction. The sooner you get serious about our cause, the sooner you will discover that Reese is heading in a right direction, not a wrong one. We are not here to hold hands. We are here to make a difference."

Tyler sat back and grumbled something in reply, sounding like little more than a petulant child. Reese continued to stare at the knife in her hand and to test its weight. She didn't bother to test how sharp it was—that, she wasn't sure she wanted to know.

"You're a born warrior," Jacob told her. "I know more about you than you might think. Your reputation in Lincoln was growing, and David sometimes talked with me. He would speak glowingly of your strength, your quickness, your mind in a fight. But you were born for this cause, not to waste your talents fighting an unending battle trying to disarm weapons instead of disarming the people who wield them. Because that is all the demons are—weapons. You were born to take up those weapons yourself and wield them in the cause of the universe, of life and strength and growth in the face of corruption and rot."

Her response was automatic, even though he was unsettling her—not only by his words, but also because his was the same voice that had spoken to her from a demonic incarnation only the night before. "I won't fight alongside demons. I won't use the demonic." She turned in her seat, trying to face him. "And you should know better by now. Even granted that you are right about some things, it was Clint who tried to teach you to use the demonic. Clint you welcomed. And look at what you know now—he was your greatest enemy all along."

"Not mine," Jacob said, flushing. "Not my enemy. Ours. The enemy of the Oneness. And I have admitted, freely, that I was wrong about him. But it was a distraction—a tactic of the enemy to knock me off course. My basic understanding was not wrong. I was simply deceived in applying it."

Their road was taking them through a stretch of orchards, apples growing on one side and an open, unplowed field of weeds waving in the other. Jacob pulled over abruptly and got out, stalking around to open Reese's door.

"What are we doing?" she asked, reaching for her crutches as Tyler handled them to her.

"I'm hungry," Jacob said.

Reese still had the knife in her hand as she slipped one crutch under her arm and used it to hop forward. It crunched and threatened to slide away on the gravel, but she kept herself upright. She wrinkled her nose. "The apples are still green."

"I wasn't thinking of eating those." He pointed down an orchard row to a chicken scratching in the dirt. "Kill that," he said.

She didn't even know why she did it—why she just obeyed, like his word was a switch that triggered a response. Without even thinking, she aimed the knife and threw it.

It killed the bird.

Uneasily, she waited as Tyler went to retrieve it. Jacob looked pleased. "That was excellent," he said. "You didn't even need time to aim. And that isn't even a throwing knife. David was right about you."

"David has never been right about me." Her snapped response surprised her with its own vehemence.

Jacob's chuckle quieted. "I'm sorry. Poor choice of words.

But you are the warrior your reputation says you are." He looked pleased—proud, even. It made her uncomfortable. Too much like he was taking ownership of her gifts.

Even so, she knew what he said was true. She was a fighter. The sword was her gift—every member of the Oneness had a special gifting in something, and battle was hers. Years with the Lincoln cell, leading others into the fray, had honed that gift until it was as sharp as the knife in her hand.

But it still chilled her to think what Jacob wanted her to do with it.

Tyler held out the chicken, and it flopped ungraciously in his hand. "What do you want to do with this?" he said.

"Gut it and pluck it and eat it," Jacob answered.

"Isn't that stealing?"

"We already killed it. Anyway, its being out here means it wandered away from the coop. The owners have probably given it up for dead anyway. Better us than a coyote."

Tyler sighed and flopped down under a tree, starting the work of gutting the bird.

"You know how to do that?" Jacob asked.

"I'm not completely useless."

Jacob didn't bother to respond.

Reese just laughed and hopped over beside Tyler, laying her crutch down on the grass as she eased down against the trunk of the tree. She could help with the next step. Chicken plucking wasn't the most pleasant task she could think of, but it wasn't the worst either.

"I don't like any of this," Tyler said quietly. "Those knives."

"He got one for you too."

"I won't use it."

"Maybe you can kill us some more chickens."

"I couldn't do what you did anyway. I'm a fisher, not a hunter."

"Where did you learn to gut a chicken?"

"Chris shoots birds once in a while."

Chris.

A pain in Reese's stomach accompanied the mention of his name.

She knew that she ought to feel guilty for running out on the cell. She knew that she ought to feel guilty for co-opting a mission, for changing course when she was supposed to be converting Jacob and considering her own conversion instead. She knew that on some level, to some degree, she was acting as a traitor.

But it was Chris she felt regret over, and Chris she wished more than anything she could talk to.

"Do you suppose he's all right?" she asked.

"He's a man. He can take care of himself."

"That's not exactly what I meant."

"Do I think he's worried sick about you? Yes. And probably about me too. I try to convince him I can take care of myself too, but he doesn't believe me." Tyler smiled, though sweat was running down his face and getting chicken feathers and dust stuck in it. "He still thinks I'm a little kid who just lost his parents and needs his help to get through life." His expression sobered. "But I wouldn't have made it without him."

"I'm sorry to worry him," Reese told him. "I wish there was some other way."

"There is some other way."

"No, there isn't. I really have to figure this out. You told me that yourself."

"I know I did. I just wish Jacob didn't have to be in the middle of it."

"I can't figure this one out without him. He's the only one asking questions."

Tyler grimaced. "David asked questions."

"What's that supposed to mean?"

"Just be careful about the answers you find, I guess."

"It's not a matter of 'being careful.' You look for the truth, and when you find it, you accept it. I don't have a choice about that."

"Okay," Tyler said.

She wanted to get up and walk off in frustration, pace up and down the orchard rows to cool her head a little, but her bad ankle made jumping up impossible, and in the heat the effort it would take to pull herself up and get on the crutch again didn't quite feel worth it.

She wished Chris was here. She wanted to talk to him. Tyler was Oneness—even if he hadn't been for long—and she couldn't help feeling like he was guarding his loyalties. Like he saw her as the potential traitor she felt like.

For the millionth time she wished David had never exiled her.

Somehow she was sure that if he hadn't, she wouldn't be where she was now. And even if where she was now was in one sense good—truth was better than a lie, always—she would have given anything to trade this life for her old one.

Chris, with his resistance to becoming One, did not share Tyler's conflict.

That evening, they roasted the bird over a fire in the orchard. The weather was clear and they planned to sleep out here. It would take another two days of driving at least to reach Lincoln, and this was nicer than some places they could end up sleeping.

Tyler climbed a tree above Reese and settled into the branches.

"You going to sleep up there?"

"Yup."

"That can't be comfortable."

"Neither can the ground. Chris and me used to do this when we were kids. We'd go camping up in the cliffs and find trees to sleep in. Don't have to worry about getting eaten by wolves."

"There are no wolves within a thousand miles of here."

"There weren't when we were kids, either. Didn't stop us from climbing the trees."

She smiled as she laid her crutch beside her and tried to get comfortable at the base of the tree. Jacob was a ways away, thinking stormy thoughts.

The knife Jacob had given her was in its sheath near her hand. It made her feel safer somehow.

She wondered how she might end up using it, other than killing chickens.

To her surprise, as she squirmed to get comfortable amidst the roots and ruts of the orchard ground, she found herself blinking away tears.

This wasn't where she wanted to be.

Thinking about killing a man.

Thinking about turning her back on everything she'd been taught and taking up arms in a way that would make everyone she loved see her as an enemy.

But if Jacob was right . . .

Truth was truth.

"Reese," Tyler said from above.

"Yeah?" She squinted up, but she couldn't see him in the shadows overhead. It had gotten late, leafy branches arced out above her, and the moon was waning—even with a clear sky, there was little light.

"You should pray," he said.

For some reason, she hadn't thought about that.

"I'm not really a praying person," she said. "I mean, I serve by fighting. Prayer is Richard's forte."

"Yeah, but it's for everyone, right? Just a way of getting in touch with the Spirit . . . with who we are." He cleared his throat. "There've been a couple of times in all this craziness when I felt pretty lost and had no idea what to do, and I tried praying. And last time I tried it, I walked."

She smiled. She would never forget that.

"You were amazing."

"It wasn't me. It was the Oneness. I just tapped into it. So . . . well, you aren't alone, even with all this."

"Tyler . . ." She struggled to put words together. "You know the things I'm thinking about. What I'm considering doing. How much of a black sheep Jacob is."

"Yes, but even if everyone else in the Oneness thinks you're wrong and you're really right, that doesn't make you cut off. The Oneness only exists because of the Spirit, right? It's the thing uniting everyone. And I don't think the Spirit takes sides. So you can't be kicked out, and you really never will be alone. Even Jacob isn't."

She thought about that. "How did you get so smart?" she asked, teasing, only half-serious. She wasn't sure she wanted to think too heavily about what he was saying.

"I've had to think a lot," Tyler said. "This Oneness business has not exactly been an easy ride so far."

"I guess not."

"First there was you, and the whole exile thing. And then right away we're getting attacked by demons, and fighting the hive, and kidnapped by Jacob and almost killed by Clint. And pretty much the whole time it's been just me and Chris, and Chris isn't even One. So I've been trying to figure out a lot of things on my feet."

There was a rustle of leaves and branches, and he dropped down in front of her, looking her in the eye. Her head and shoulders were propped up against the tree, and she felt tears in her eyes as he looked at her.

"I know this is hard," he said. "But you aren't alone. And you're right—the truth is out there. I don't think Jacob is leading you to it. But as long as it's really what you care about most—finding the truth, and really being Oneness, whatever that means—you'll be okay. Just make sure it's what you care about most."

She impatiently wiped a tear away with the heel of her hand. "I'm not sure what you're saying."

"Think about it."

"I will."

She wouldn't. Now right now. There was too much to think about.

Tyler pulled himself back up into the tree, and Reese closed her eyes and settled down at its base.

Just for a little while, she didn't want to think at all.

That night Richard found himself a perch on the roof and sat staring out at the lights on the bay. A barely-there sliver of moon hung over the sea; the water beneath was deep black and still.

"And the earth was without form and void," he said to himself, "and the Spirit of God hovered on the face of the waters."

He turned his head at the sound of a window opening, and April clambered out onto the roof, closing the window quietly so as not to wake Nick, who slept beside it. She settled next to Richard.

"Hey," she said.

"Hey."

"You're in my spot."

He smiled. "It's a free country."

"So how was your time with Julie?"

"It was fine. The children ran around with Miranda in the backyard, and Julie was about as open as anyone I've ever known. She's scared—has some reason to be, since they think she's the one who gave the trucker the dose that killed him—but I think she's going to be all right. We stopped for a talk with Lieutenant Jackson as well, and it sounds like they think Julie was an ignorant accomplice. If anyone killed the man on purpose it was Jacob or his wife."

April shook her head. "Don't know why they would do that. He wasn't a threat to them."

"Who knows what they see as a threat?"

April was quiet. Then, "Maybe Reese does, by now."

"I should have . . ."

He let it trail off. She pushed. "You should have what?"

"I should have thought more carefully before I gave Reese the job of dealing with Jacob. Should have thought about how vulnerable she was. Is."

"It's not your fault," April said.

"Maybe it is."

"You just took down a hive," April answered. "Destroyed a threat to all of us. Stripped a sorcerer of his power, saved a kid from demon possession, got us all through alive."

"Thank you for your kindness, but you got yourselves through alive. And I lost one kid. And we didn't turn David. And . . ."

"If you blame yourself for Melissa, I might smack you."

He looked at her, barely able to make out her fine features

in the scant light. She was pale and slender, fragile in a setting like this—the combination of tough and vulnerable that April had always been.

"I was thinking of doing that, yes," he said.

"Melissa was already dying before she came," April said. "You saved her in the only way that really counts."

"But the children . . ."

"You really think the hive was going to keep helping her? They were just using her, like they use everybody else. They would have finished with her and then let the cancer take over, and she would have died a traitor and knowing she'd been deceived and done terrible things because of it. You saved her from that, Richard."

He thought it over and swallowed a lump in his throat. "Thank you."

"No problem."

The night was still, so still they could hear gentle waves lapping in the harbour below. The air was still warm, but a cool breeze off the water made it more than tolerable.

"So what do we do about Reese?" April asked.

"Nothing."

"Nothing?"

"Our offensive is over. We won. Reese still has a mission to finish, and she'll finish it. We can't do anything else but wait for her. And trust her."

April bit her lip. "You think we can?"

"Yes," Richard said slowly.

"Good. I think so too."

They sat, side by side in the darkness, for an hour or more.

Finally April asked, "You planning to sit out here all night?"

"I considered it."

"You should sleep."

"So should you."

She threw something off the roof—a twig or piece of debris she'd been playing with. "I don't need sleep. Slept for weeks after the cave."

Neither of them went to bed.

* * * * *

Two hundred miles away, Chris was sleeping under the stars in the back of his pickup truck.

He woke to the sound of a coyote howling and yipping not far away. A gun in the truck bed beside him calmed him, and he tossed in his sleeping bag and tried to get comfortable enough to sleep again.

The pressure was growing.

He could feel it in the air, like a storm front. Weight, heat, building, suffocating him.

He knew what it was.

He tossed again, lying on his back now, staring up at the stars. The coyote launched into a series of barks and yelps, joined by several others.

He wouldn't give in.

Not yet.

Not this way.

A memory had been preying on his mind: the hermit on Tempter's Mountain, before he was shot to death by David, telling him, "Don't wait too long."

He didn't know how long "too long" was, but he was determined to wait.

No matter how strongly the Spirit pushed on him to surrender, he was not ready to go under yet.

He couldn't breathe. The coyotes were getting louder. Cursing, he tossed off his bedding, grabbed his gun, and jumped out of the truck onto the hard dirt. Might as well go hunting. Quiet things down.

But it was too dark.

Cursing again, he got into his truck and turned it on, headlights flooding the night. The landscape ahead of him was barren; dirt and gravel, mostly; scrub, low trees. The lights picked up a pair of eyes that glowed green back at him and then loped away.

The coyotes quieted down.

He hadn't realized they were that close.

Breathing harder, he turned the engine and lights off, climbed back into the truck bed, and lay down on his back.

There were stars, but their light was too distant to make any difference down here. The moon was almost nonexistent.

"Reese, blast you," he whispered. "Where are you?"

If he was Oneness, maybe he would have some supernatural way of finding her. He could reach out and . . .

Well, who knew what he could do.

He wasn't Oneness. Unlike his mother, his best friend, and the girl he was pretty sure he loved.

He had waited a week for her to come home or be in touch and then had decided to go out and find her. Patience was not his strong suit, and he could not celebrate their victory over the hive—if victory it really was—without her. His whole journey with the Oneness had begun because of Reese. As far as he was concerned, if she wasn't home and healed, they hadn't won anything.

He sat up, leaned against the rear window of his truck, and stared out at his desert surroundings. He had gone to the corrective facility where Reese and Tyler had collected Jacob and tried to follow them from there, heading off in the initial direction Lieutenant Jackson indicated and then asking around. The trio was distinctive enough to remember, especially with Jacob a part of them—the man was like a magnet; no one could fail to be affected by the pull he gave off. But while a few people remembered seeing them and could point him in the right direction—a gas station attendant, a grocer—there were just too many possibilities and not enough pointers to get him all the way to them. The one thing he was fairly sure they had done was go back to the site where Clint had killed the police officers who pulled him over on the side of the highway. They had gone in that direction, and gut instinct told him they had stopped there.

That must have been hell for Tyler.

Tyler.

He wouldn't really be happy until Tyler was home, either.

From there he had decided on a different tack, and gone to the Lincoln cell to see if they had any idea who Reese might have contacted or where she might have gone. They looked at him like he had two heads when he asked if she had family—not a normal question for Oneness, then. But someone thought that Reese was originally from the mountains a few days' north and east of them. Someone there might know her.

So. Where else did he have to go?

He heard something.

He quieted his thoughts and concentrated on listening, just to be sure.

Yes, there it was again.

The coyotes coming back?

Softly, slowly, he reached for his gun.

Had the air grown heavier?

Chris was not one who needed his hand held, but right now he wished Tyler was here. Another set of eyes and ears would come in handy.

Especially a set that could better sense things beyond what was strictly earthly.

The sound—a scratching, movement, gravel crunching—was growing closer.

And he didn't think it was the coyotes.

"Tyler," he whispered, "you picked a ba-a-d time to disappear."

Keeping his weight carefully balanced, he pushed himself so he was squatting, ready to jump up, react, move. He readied his gun to fire.

And hoped whatever was out there was actually susceptible to bullets.

Eyes. There were eyes staring at him again, glowing—only this time they weren't picking up the light from his headlights.

He stared back, wishing he could see what he was looking at and wondering if the creature thought the same or if it could see what he couldn't—if its eyesight in the dark was as good as his was nonexistent.

With his gun cocked, he held it for a long two minutes aimed at the eyes, but they did not move, and he did not fire. His hands wanted to shake, but he held them steady.

Slowly, he lowered the barrel.

He crouched, keeping his eyes on the gleaming eyes before him, and felt around his sleeping bag for the heavy-duty flashlight he knew was there somewhere. His hand closed around it, and quickly, he raised himself and flicked the light on so he could see what was there.

He nearly dropped the light.

It went out. He pounded the bottom of the metal tube, jarring the battery back into working order, but this time the beam caught nothing.

The glowing eyes were gone.

The figure he had seen watching him from the desert was gone.

But he knew what his own eyes had seen standing there.

A child.

Julie woke to the sound of conflict outside. Voices raised, a door slamming. A car starting and tires squealing as it tore away.

She hated it. Not just the noise pulling her out of sleep, but the tension, the anger, and the loneliness that throbbed in the silence of her room when the noises died down again.

The safe house was in a relatively quiet part of the city, but still minor conflicts like this happened, and never failed to wake her. She didn't know why they always seemed to come at night. Like brokenness and anger and drunkenness and everything else that manifested itself here waited for the darkness, or the glow of streetlights, to come out and show itself.

Times like this, she missed the farm. No matter how bad things had gotten there, no matter how much Jacob had betrayed them, she'd been searching for a better life there, and most days it seemed like she'd found it. She and everyone else who pitched their lot in with Jacob and his wife and the community. They wanted to create a place where life happened in the day, and all that came out at night were sweet dreams, innocent and hearty and fed by home-cooked food and wholesome relationships and a hard day's work.

Was it so much to ask, that life could be like that? That you could go to bed with a clean conscience and sleep to the sound of insects buzzing in the corn and wake to a sunrise and chickens and smiles from people you liked and trusted?

She'd wanted life to be like that for Miranda's sake, too. Even more so than for herself. She'd wanted her daughter to grow up in a world that wasn't so bitter, that didn't taste like car exhaust and acid rain. She wanted Miranda to be like girls in the past, in books about growing up on the prairies or on safe, protected, happy islands. And Miranda was like those girls.

At least, she was until her mother killed a man.

So much for clean conscience.

It was an accident, she told herself in the darkness of her room. Outside another door slammed and more tires squealed, and she found tears on her face.

An accident.

She had only been trying to help care for him. Just following Lorrie's directions . . .

Such a terrible end to the story. And it was a story she'd given up so much for . . . sacrificed more than she wanted to remember.

She rolled over, clutching her pillow, and tried hard to fall back asleep. Didn't want to be awake right now. Didn't want to think.

A scream from outside jolted her out of bed.

Was that Miranda?

She grabbed a sweater from a hook by the bedroom door and rushed out, ignoring protocol—she wasn't supposed to go outside with letting the house supervisor know. The air outside was cold—strange after weeks of high heat. It pierced her through as she stepped into the artificial, harshly lit world of the city outdoors. Shadows darting across the street drew her attention to something happening over there—and she heard the scream again.

It was Miranda.

What was she doing out here? How had she gotten out without anyone knowing?

Jacob had always said the world was a dangerous place.

How had her daughter plunged straight into the middle of it only weeks after leaving the safety of the community?

As Julie rushed across the asphalt street, under the hanging lights to the shadows beyond, calling her daughter's name and straining to see something, anything, clearly, she felt as though hands were grasping at her and someone was trying to pull her back.

Voices, all in her head, clamoured—Stop, turn around. Don't go there. Don't . . .

A blinding light cut off the shadows and the voices simultaneously.

* * * * *

When Chris woke in the morning, he searched around the truck and found coyote tracks alarmingly close in the dirt, but no sign of the child. No footprints, nothing.

One part of his mind, the part that was pretending the world still operated on normal rules, berated him for not trying to find the child the night before. A kid, that part of his mind told him. Lost in the desert. What kind of scared, selfish idiot wouldn't go out searching until he rescued him? The kid was lost, or a runaway, definitely not safe out there in the night with the coyotes still near and who knew what other dangers lurking.

The other part of his mind dismissed all that and said the child wasn't just a kid, wasn't just a runaway, wasn't part of this world at all. That part of his mind told him that he'd seen something that belonged to the world of the angels and the demons and the Oneness, and he would never have found him even if he'd searched all night, and if he had found him, the child would not have needed his help.

What the child wanted, he did not know. But he believed this part of his mind, and not the part that was chiding him for refusing to leave the truck. He'd spent the rest of the night sitting up with his back against the window, his shotgun cradled between his legs, and the flashlight close at hand.

He had no desire to revisit that night, or to spend another one like it out here.

But he really had no idea what to do now. A night full of terrors and watchers wasn't much better than a day with little direction, a day he would spend trying to hunt Reese down in an area where she was almost certain not to be.

He finished his third circuit around the truck, wider this

Rachel Starr Thomson

time than the others, looking for any sign of the child he knew hadn't left signs. The sun was already growing hot, and he could feel sweat raising on the back of his neck. He wiped it with his hand and growled, wishing Tyler was here to grumble at.

Maybe he should call the village. Talk to Richard. Tell him what he'd seen and ask him if he had any idea what it was.

"No," he said out loud.

He didn't really want to get the cell into this.

When he found Reese, he needed to talk to her, and it needed to be just the two of them—well, and Tyler. Sort of. But it needed to be about them, not about the cell.

Even if he was pretty lost without them right now.

He packed up his things and started the truck again, heading north. He didn't really know what he thought he was doing. Like if he just kept following scant hopes, he'd stumble across Reese. More likely he'd get himself on the wrong road and they'd miss each other for the rest of their lives.

But he couldn't stand the thought of going home to the village and just waiting.

Better to run in circles until the day he died.

He switched the radio on as he drove, trying to ignore a growing pressure in the back of his head. The highway was clear, not many people out this far in the middle of nowhere. Old classic rock tunes blared through speakers that were in much better shape than the ones in his old truck—he almost missed the way the old radio had rattled out the bass lines. Driving a new truck made him feel uncomfortably like a new person.

The pressure was getting stronger.

He jacked the radio up louder, but the noise only seemed to make it worse—like it was clashing with some other sound and the combined effect was giving him a headache. He switched it off and drove in silence before pulling over to the side of the road and swearing.

He shoved his door open and got out, yelling, "Would you leave me alone?"

There was no answer. Naturally. What did he think was bothering him, anyway?

The Spirit.

The Oneness.

The SOMETHING that wanted him to be part of it and had decided to get aggressive about the fact.

"No," he said, stalking circles around the truck. "No, not now. I'm not ready. I need . . ."

He didn't know what he needed.

He stopped short.

The child was sitting on the hood of the truck.

This time he saw him clearly. A boy, about eleven. White-blond hair. Green eyes. Faded cheeks. An expression far more serious than most eleven year olds ever carried.

Chris blinked, and the boy was gone.

"What are you trying to do to me?" he asked.

No answer.

No apparition this time, either.

He got back in the truck and leaned his forehead against the steering wheel until it got too hot and stuffy to sit there anymore. The pressure had eased off a bit, just like last night—like seeing the child diffused it. Like lightning in a storm.

He flicked the radio back on.

And went ashen.

The news was playing.

"No," he whispered. "God, no. Please let them be wrong."

*   *   *   *   *

Richard had no idea anything was wrong until he arrived on the safe house street in Lincoln. He hadn't called ahead—figured it would be okay just to drop in and see if Julie was available for a visit. But as he pulled onto the street, he knew from the police cars everywhere and the caution tape blocking off the entire lot that something terrible had happened.

As he drew closer, he knew what it was. His gut told him.

He could feel the residue of death.

Julie.

April made a noise beside him, and without saying a word or checking on Nick and Alicia in the backseat, Richard pulled a U-turn and started to drive away.

"Why?" April asked softly.

"I don't know."

"Can't we . . ."

"Not with the children." He kept his voice low.

"You can't what?" Nick asked. "You can do whatever you want. We don't care."

He grunted as Alicia apparently elbowed him in the ribs. "Yes, we do."

Richard checked the rearview and saw the expression on Alicia's face. It figured she would be more perceptive than Nick on this front—she was Oneness where he was not, and before that, she had been possessed.

She knew both sides of this coin.

"We're getting out of here," Richard said, trying to reassure her. "Going back to the village right now."

"What happened?" Nick whined.

Richard was going to say "I'll tell you later," but Alicia spoke first. "Someone died."

Nick went quiet and still. "Oh."

"I think it was him," Alicia said, her voice shaking. "I think it was Clint. I think he did it. He killed somebody."

"Don't worry," Richard said. "They can't get back into you. You're Oneness now. The demons can't possess you ever again. And Clint isn't going to find you."

He glanced over at April, who was half-turned in her seat and was staring back at the caution-taped crime scene with a pale face. "What about the daughter?" she asked.

Miranda.

He almost hit the brake and turned around again. But he couldn't. He couldn't take the kids back there. Not when the sense of evil was still so strong in the air.

"We'll go back for her."

"You think they'll let us near her?"

"I don't know. Maybe not to take her with us. But Jackson trusts us. He'll let us visit her at least. Be some . . ."

"I'm not sure there is any comfort for this."

A muscle in April's jaw was twitching. Richard wanted to reach out and lay a comforting hand on her arm, but he needed both hands to hold the wheel. They were shaking, and he was getting less confident of his ability to keep driving.

He hadn't known Julie well. Not well at all. They had only met a tiny handful of times. She was new to the Oneness. She was a helpful contact and witness and their one link to Reese and Jacob, and Richard had looked forward to knowing her better and calling her family.

But he felt her death like it had been his own sister. Like they had known each other for years. Grief and fear pounded through him and threatened to wrestle his hands away from the wheel and send them right into an accident. Grief and fear and guilt.

They should have stopped this.

They should have known she was in danger.

They should have . . .

"We should have done something," April said.

Nick started to pipe up from the backseat again, but Alicia cut him off with another well-placed elbow.

"We'll get the kids home," Richard said. "We'll get the kids home, and then we'll figure out where to go from there."

* * * * *

The only good in the news report of Julie's murder was that Chris was fairly sure he knew where to find Reese now.

She would go to Julie's daughter. No question of that.

So he broke his silence and called the village cell. Talked to his mother and made her promise not to tell any of the others. A promise which, despite how tightly in cahoots with the rest of the Oneness she was these days, he was still able to extract from her. Old habits died hard, and Diane had stood against her own cell for a long, long time. She told him where to find the safe house where Julie and Miranda had been and gave him contact information for the lieutenant they had been working with, and then he headed for Lincoln as fast as his new truck would drive.

Which was impressively fast.

A side benefit to speeding as insanely as he was, through the bright morning sun toward the city that was far too many miles away, was that he almost felt like he could outrun the pressure. The ache that kept starting up in the back of his head and then pressing down on him like an incessant wave, the sense of being pushed to his knees that he was beginning to think of as a call.

He knew that was what it was—a voice beyond voices calling to him, trying to pull him in, trying to force his hand.

But the more it tried, the more he wanted to resist.

And then without warning he slammed his brakes, sending the truck careening as he tried to keep control of it, and pulled to the side and pounded on the steering wheel.

"Enough!" he shouted. "What are you doing to me?"

There was nothing there now. He was screaming at an empty horizon.

But he'd seen the child again. Two seconds ago, perched on the hood of his truck with the wind whipping through his hair and clothes, kneeling on one knee and staring intently at Chris.

He got out and stomped around, crunching gravel under his feet, smelling the hot-tar smell of a newly touched-up highway under the late summer sun.

There was no sign of the child now. He was going crazy.

No, he wasn't, he corrected himself. This was the Oneness, doing this to him.

What was he seeing?

He forced himself to stop pacing and calm his breathing. He had to think about this. The Oneness were people; they didn't just appear out of nowhere and disappear again just as fast, and they couldn't just kneel on the hood of a pickup truck going eighty miles an hour. Nobody could do that.

His brain ransacked what he knew of the Oneness. The cloud. That was what his mind came up with: the cloud. The dead people who were still sticking around somehow, part of the Oneness even after they'd died. Tyler had seen a member of the cloud before he'd become Oneness. This had to be the same thing. The Oneness was stalking him and sending that creepy little kid to do it.

He got back in his car, still breathing hard. The kid wasn't creepy, actually—not at all. He was a beautiful child. Nothing in his appearance or the way he looked at Chris was intrinsically frightening. It was just the way he kept showing up, and the intensity in his eyes.

Chris laid his head on the steering wheel and groaned. "I don't have time for this," he said out loud. "I need to find Reese while I still have a chance. I can't deal with ghosts right now. Please, leave me alone for a few hours, okay? Or days. Just leave me alone."

Nothing happened. No response, no feeling of calm, no ghostly apparition nodding its head.

Good enough.

He started the truck back up again and got back on the road, driving just a bit more slowly this time. Darn kid had nearly given him a heart attack. The sight of him perched up there while Chris was speeding so dangerously had made him think he might end up killing him by accident.

At least he had settled that the kid was a ghost. You couldn't kill ghosts.

* * * * *

They heard the news playing on the radio inside a truck stop where they got gas. Julie was dead.

Murdered.

Like a big, flashing neon sign with Jacob's name written on it.

He had been right.

Tyler regretted every stupid word he had said. Every challenge to Jacob's integrity and heart. Every insinuation that he didn't care about his people, that he was only using them. He could see it burned in Jacob's eyes now, pounding in his temples. He cared. He felt this. This was not just about revenge. He wanted to stop the man before another innocent person got hurt.

Tyler, for the first time, felt that he understood and wanted the same thing Jacob did.

As he walked miserable circles around the pavement, waiting until Reese and Jacob said it was time to go, his memories from the highway kept buzzing around in his head. Clint—Bertoller—and the destruction he delighted in.

Jacob was right. It was wrong to let someone like that go on living. Indefensible, even.

Memories of the farm community kept swirling around in there, too. Of their innocence and naivete. Of the way they just wanted to escape the dangers of the world and live a better, cleaner, happier life.

So much for that.

He tried to comfort himself by reminding himself that Julie had become Oneness before she died. So she would be part of the cloud now. Still One with them. Not really gone.

It was interesting to speculate about, but offered no comfort at all.

They knew now where Bertoller had recently been—in Lincoln, in time to kill Julie and set the news buzzing. That had been last night. He had left no evidence of where he would go next, at least not that the news was telling.

"Keep heading for Lincoln," Jacob said tersely when they were all three back in the car. "He was there. We have no choice but to start looking for him there."

"You can't go to the crime scene," Reese said from behind the wheel. "They'll arrest you."

"Better you don't show your face either," Jacob said.

"I'll go," Tyler said from the backseat.

Driving as fast and hard as they could, it would be a day and a half before they reached the scene of the crime. By that time any evidence might have vanished. But there was nothing else they could do.

Reese said the words. "It's going to be another day before we can make it."

"There's another way to travel," Jacob said. "A faster way."

Reese swallowed hard. "No."

"I know how to reach them," he went on. "How to get their help. They can get us there in minutes."

"I won't work with demons."

"We don't have days!"

She turned and met his gaze, her own remarkably steady. "Julie is already dead, Jacob. Getting there faster won't stop that."

He sat back and turned his face away. "If anyone else dies before we get there, their blood is on your head."

She flinched.

"Wait," Tyler said.

"What?" Reese asked, twisting her head back a little to see him while she drove.

"The way demons can travel—are they the only ones who can do that? I mean, I've been able to do some pretty crazy stuff."

"You walked, Tyler."

"Yeah, but I did it while paralysed. That's not so shabby, is it? I'm just saying, it seems like as Oneness, we should have access to more . . . power. Than we do."

"The boy is on the right track," Jacob said.

"I'm not talking about working with demons. Or turning into vigilantes. I'm just saying, we're supposed to be something more than human, right? Are we really stuck driving in cars?"

"I don't know," Reese said. "If there is another way to do this, I don't know it. Or how to do it."

"Richard might."

"I can't call them."

Tyler sighed. "All right."

The highway left behind a wooded stretch and opened to a mountain vista that spread before them. It should have been breathtaking. Instead, it merely looked like an obstacle—hours upon hours expressed in space. Hours in which Bertoller might strike, someone might die, they might lose.

Tyler offered a mute prayer to the Spirit and hoped their efforts would end in some kind of success. The prayer went silent into the air, yet he had a sense that it wasn't unheard.

He had walked under the power of the Spirit. Why couldn't he fly under the same power?

Smiling a little, he closed his eyes and experimented. Reached out with his mind and heart and tried to touch something.

To his surprise, he did.

He felt, in a way that was unmistakable though not strictly

tangible, a warmth—and a pulse.

Automatically, he reached out with his hands and felt himself taking something into them—the image that formed in his mind was one of gathering a horse's mane and filling his fists with it, and then leaning over the arched neck of the beast—

And flames, his hands were full of flames, the air was full of fire, but he did not burn.

He heard Reese shout, startled, "Tyler!"

He opened his eyes.

They were flying.

Beneath him he could make out the shape of a horse with a mane and tail of fire, its legs pounding a path through the air, the world beneath streaking past so fast it was a blur. He couldn't see Jacob or Reese—his eyes were too full of fire. But they were there.

His heart raced until it wanted to burst.

And he heard Reese's voice again—more urgent this time, now scared, now terrified. "Tyler!"

He looked down.

She was falling toward the earth.

* * * * *

Reese plunged through the air, her eyes full of tears as the wind tore at her face and hair and clothes. The earth rapidly approached from below.

One thought passed through her mind.

She would never avenge Patrick. Never keep her promise. Never redeem herself.

Something jerked her up, suspending her in the air. Her eyes were too full of saline and water to see what it was. Her rescuer lowered her to the earth by the folds of her shirt until her feet touched ground, and her knees buckled with fear and adrenaline.

What had Tyler just done?

And why had she fallen?

She wiped her eyes with her sleeve and looked up, scanning the sky as her vision cleared. Blue sky, cloud streaked, no sign of flaming horses or flying men or of her rescuer.

When she lowered her eyes again, though, her rescuer was crouched on the ground before her—a spirit inhabiting the body of a raven with a fox's head.

Trembling overtook her. "Why?" she asked. "Why did you help me?"

In answer, the creature simply bowed its head.

Jacob was right.

It was offering itself as her servant.

"No," she whispered. Her sword was forming in her hand, but only halfway—as though it knew it wasn't wanted. The dead bear haunted her. She felt, in some way that she couldn't explain, that she should not have killed it. Evil it might be, but it had helped her—had done her a service she asked it for.

It had served her, as she had requested that it do, and she had killed it to cover her own sin.

"Go," she said, gathering all the strength she could into her voice and directing it at the creature. "Leave me."

It looked up, its eyes unnervingly full of intelligence. "If you do not want us," it said, "why do you call for us?"

"I don't!"

"You do," it said.

And with a flap of its black wings, it flew away.

She watched it go and then stopped to take in her surroundings. She was in a desert. Twisted thorn trees and low ground scrub grew from sandy, rocky ground. Low hills surrounded her on every side. She suspected she was lost in the terrain somewhere between Lincoln and the mountains to the north, but other than that, she might as well have been on Mars for all she knew where to go from here.

"Great," she muttered.

She could, of course, call for the demons and ask them to get her out of here.

They'd been rather helpful so far.

"Blast it," she snapped. "Stop it, Reese."

But what was she supposed to do now?

* * * * *

Tyler didn't know if he simply lost his grip or if the horse bucked him off. He did know that he found himself pelting through the air toward a body of water, which he hit clumsily.

Salt. He'd come home.

He swam to the surface and burst into sunlit air. A few feet away, Jacob was gasping for breath. The shore was an easy swim away, and Tyler struck out for it automatically, calling to Jacob to follow him.

Tyler reached the beach with Jacob on his heels, and as he staggered onto shore, Jacob grabbed his shoulder, swung him around, and punched him fully in the face.

Tyler went down, blood spurting from his nose and pain splitting through his head. Jacob stood over him panting like a bull, his knees bent in a fighter's stance, waiting for Tyler to rise and fight him.

Tyler decided that was unwise.

"What are you doing?" he shouted through the pain, hoping his words were intelligible.

"Where is she?" Jacob roared.

"Reese? I don't know! I didn't lose her!"

Jacob went for a kick, and Tyler rolled away and got warily to his feet, keeping his distance.

"I don't want to fight you," he said.

"Of course you don't," Jacob shot back. "You're a weakling and a coward. And a fool. What were you thinking back there?"

"I was thinking we could get to Lincoln faster," Tyler said. "You wanted to!"

"You're playing with powers you don't understand," Jacob raged, "and you've lost her—she's my best hope for justice, and you've lost her. Maybe killed her. Are you proud of yourself?"

Tyler's rising anger was checked when he realized Jacob's eyes were full of tears, and he remembered the man's response to Julie's death.

"I'm sorry," he said, still keeping his distance. Jacob seemed to be relaxing a little—he hoped. He touched his face, inspecting. His nose wasn't broken, although his eye was swelling and he was sure he looked a bloody mess.

"Look," Tyler said, "I don't know what happened to Reese, but you beating me up isn't going to help us find her."

"Where are we?" Jacob asked, suddenly switching tacks. He looked around him wildly. "Do you know this area?"

"Maybe," Tyler said, taking in the ocean, the beach, and the dunes. The sweeping cliffs of home were missing—this wasn't his coast. "Not sure," he confessed. "But I'm guessing we're still north of Lincoln, so if we just keep the ocean to our right, we'll head the right way." He paused, his thoughts going in multiple directions. "Why did we fall?"

Jacob didn't try to answer that. His voice was still choked with anger. "That would help if we knew Reese went to Lincoln."

"She fell just before we did," Tyler said. "Maybe she's nearby."

"Do you have any idea how fast we were travelling?" Jacob shot back.

"We . . . no."

"Then you have no way to say how close she might be. Or how far."

Tyler wiped the blood from his face and grimaced. Jacob had an amazing ability to make him feel like something scraped off someone's shoe.

Jacob regarded him with an expression somewhere between aggression and cunning. "Well," he said when Tyler had finished wiping most of the blood from his face and staunching the blood flow with his sleeve, "you got us into this, holy boy. Get us out."

Tyler stared at him. Behind them, waves washed up calmly on the shore, rolling in rhythmically from a calm sea. "I can't," he said finally.

"You called up horses of fire to transport us through the air. Find Reese."

Tyler found himself assailed with confusion. "I didn't . . . I didn't do that."

Jacob raised his eyebrow. "Then who did?"

"Um. The Spirit."

"Then tell the Spirit to find Reese."

"I don't tell the Spirit what to do." His cheeks flushed hot.

"A lot of good you are, then," Jacob said. His eyes were flaring dangerously. He turned and began to stalk up the beach—purposefully. Tyler watched him go for a few minutes, then started to run after him when Jacob turned inland and started up the dunes.

"Wait!" he called. "What are you going to do?"

He thought he knew the answer to that question.

Jacob was going to do what he'd been urging Reese to do.

He was going to call on the demons.

Julie woke to the sound of a clock ticking. She was lying on something cool and soft and damp—moss.

She opened her eyes. A canopy of leaves and branches overhead rustled as a pair of goldfinches flickered through it.

The ticking was her own watch.

She checked it. Four o'clock in the afternoon.

What afternoon, she didn't know.

She didn't sit up. She was gripped by an irrational fear that if she tried to move, she would discover some terrible injury. This despite the fact that as she lay there, she felt no pain, nothing wrong—just peace and restful comfort.

But the fear wasn't irrational, she remembered. It was entirely rational, because she had been shot. Hadn't she?

And the men who did it had been holding knives and were leering at her with promises in their eyes that she didn't care to remember.

So where in the world—

And what—

"I'm dead," she said out loud. "This is the cloud."

Maybe. But then why could she hear her watch ticking?

She closed her eyes again and tried to remember. She remembered Miranda's screams, and going into the night to try to save her—but Miranda hadn't been there. She'd only found the men, and felt an undeniable demonic presence in the air, and they had been brandishing those knives and one of the men had shot her.

Could she remember the bullet hitting?

That was a stupid question, she told herself. He had fired at almost point-blank range. There was absolutely no way he had missed.

One way to settle that, she decided. She lifted her head and opened her eyes and inspected herself. She was still wearing long pajamas and a sweater. The cuffs of her striped pajama pants were a little dirty—from running across the street, she supposed. There was no blood, no tears in the fabric, no bullet holes.

She was fairly sure she wasn't dead and still in pajamas.

But there was something in her memory. A moment—an encounter—death.

She sat up slowly. Nothing hurt. She reached for her feet and stretched. The goldfinches overhead had been joined by a second pair, flashing in and out of the branches overhead.

And something else.

Something else was up there.

She focused her eyes on the branches, trying to catch it—trying to see clearly what was just teasing at the edges of her vision. Glints of light, movement. The more she tried to focus, the harder it was to see. She stood slowly, wanting to get closer, and the birds flew away, leaving bobbing branches behind them.

A rustling behind her made her whirl around.

Nothing.

She was in the woods. Trees, not too thick, surrounded her on every side, letting in golden and green light from above. The ground was mossy in places, stony in others. Although the trees overhead and on every side were mostly deciduous, the air smelled heavily of pine. The whole feel of the woods was friendly. It might be any stretch of land in cottage country, welcoming and probably not far from water. Except for her bizarre memories—and the fact that she had been in Lincoln at night last she knew—nothing about this place was threatening.

Something rustled again—this time on the other side. She wheeled around once more and this time saw a movement of light in the trees.

What was she seeing?

She closed her eyes. Concentrated on breathing slowly, methodically. Somehow she felt that whatever presence was here with her, she would not see it with her eyes alone.

A voice spoke into the silence of her heart.

Hello.

"Who are you?" she whispered.

You know.

"How did I get here?"

I brought you.

"Why?"

She opened her eyes. The presence was still invisible, but as she listened for the voice again, she felt a sense of someone smiling.

And the voice said:

I have a plan.

* * * * *

When Chris reached the safe house, the street was blocked off on both sides with caution tape. A squad car with its lights going sat at one end. He parked a street over and walked to the scene, looking for Lieutenant Jackson.

He spotted the man talking to a couple of other officers across the street from the house. Chris raised his hand to get his attention as he approached.

A woman officer cut off his approach. "Where do you think you're going?"

"I need to talk to the lieutenant," Chris said. "I can help . . ."

Jackson walked up behind the woman, making further bluffing unnecessary. "I'll talk to this young man," he said, dismissing her with his tone. She backed off, and Jackson lowered his voice—its vehemence undeniable despite the lower volume.

"What are you doing here? Where's your girlfriend?"

"I was hoping you could tell me that."

"She took off with my star prisoner," the lieutenant said.

"You let her."

"She was supposed to come back by now. Instead she called and told me nothing helpful. At the time I was still willing to play along, but things have changed. I traced the call back to a pay phone a few days' drive up north, but we haven't been able to track them down. I need that guy back here, now, or you know what's going to hit the fan."

"I'm sorry," Chris said, taken aback. "I don't know where she is. I thought she would come here when she heard about the . . . the murder."

Hope flashed in Jackson's eyes. "You think she will?"

"She cares about these people," Chris said. "She'll come for Miranda."

The look on Jackson's face grew darker. "I wish I could say she'd find her."

"What do you mean?"

"The kid's gone."

"What?"

Jackson growled. "Listen, kid, this is off the record. You understand? I am telling you because you and your kind have made this hot water hotter, and if there's anything you can do to help me, you owe it to me by now."

"Agreed," Chris said, not bothering to correct Jackson's perception. The Oneness were not his kind. But they did owe the man something.

"The kid is gone," Jackson repeated. "She disappeared last night. Your girlfriend's got nothing to see here."

"She might need to see the body," Chris said.

"Good luck."

That one caught him completely off guard. "What? What do you mean?"

"We don't have that either."

"What are you talking about? The news said Julie had been murdered."

"I know what the news said. It said what we told them—and as far as we know, it's true. We found blood—hers—and a murder weapon, and we've got an eyewitness—neighbourhood kid—who saw her get shot at point-blank. What we don't got is a body."

"The murderers took it?"

"Not according to the eyewitness, they didn't."

"Then what?" Chris asked. "It got up and walked off by itself?"

"Under normal circumstances, my best guess would be that the killers came back and took the body to dispose of it. But scouring the usual places has turned up nothing so far. All we've got is a witness who saw someone killed and the killers run away, leaving the body, and then no body. And these aren't normal circumstances. As I don't have to tell you."

"And Miranda?" Chris asked. "Did anyone see what happened to her?"

"No. Somehow she got taken from the house without any

of the guards noticing. And the kid who saw the murder didn't see a girl."

Chris frowned. "Maybe she just ran off. Heard something, saw something, got scared."

"Either way, we're looking for her."

Chris nodded. The conversation hadn't left him much room to process the fact that Reese wasn't here.

But she would come. She'd be here. The murder was all over the news; she'd have to hear about it. And from the reports he'd heard, the media didn't know that the body was missing, or that Miranda was.

If Reese knew that, she might not come here at all, leaving Chris without a lead once again. A thought he hated.

"So," Jackson said, spreading his feet and folding his arms, "What can I do for you?"

"I need to find Reese."

"You and me both."

"I think she'll come here. If you can just give me some kind of authorization to hang around . . ."

"Suits me," Jackson said. "I'd rather have you waiting for her here than somewhere I can't keep an eye on you. I might as well tell you, because you seem like an intelligent man, that your girlfriend is two steps away from some serious hot water. Jacob is suspect number one in this murder. If Reese doesn't bring him back, she's going to look like an accomplice."

Chris nodded. "I understand."

"You tell me if she shows up."

"I'll do the right thing," Chris said, and added, "sir."

Jackson looked him hard in the eye. "I believe you will. Just make sure the right thing is right for all of us. Stick around, if you like. Don't touch anything."

The lieutenant went back to work, and Chris wandered up the street. The air was remarkably cooler today—like autumn had suddenly come into the area, unannounced but more than welcome. The houses were quiet. He guessed at least some folks had vacated.

Stepping back onto someone's lawn, he surveyed the scene. The safe house was across the street from a dark alley where most of the cops were concentrated—the murder site, he guessed. The house to the left sported a window looking down on the scene. Must be where the witness had been.

On an impulse, he crossed the street to the house, looked around to make sure he wasn't being noticed—the cops were ignoring him—and knocked.

The door cracked open immediately, just long enough for whoever was on the other side to get a good look at him—and then the door opened and the person practically hauled him inside and shut the door behind them.

Slightly bewildered, Chris found himself facing an old woman with a small boy tucked behind her. "Uh, hi," he said. "I'm—"

"You're not a cop, are you?" the woman asked.

"No."

"Sit down," she said, waving at him to sit. He lowered himself cautiously onto a love seat. The living room was crowded and dark, the street blocked out by dusty blinds and stacks of paper and other clutter. He didn't get the feeling that this woman ever really let the sun in. "Sonny," she said to the boy, "go get this man a drink."

Chris started to protest, but the boy was already off to the kitchen. He folded his hands in his lap, uncomfortably aware that the woman was scrutinizing everything about him.

"Why did you bring me in here?" he asked.

"Why did you knock on my door?" she shot back. Her quickness surprised him.

"I wanted to talk to whoever saw the murder last night," Chris said. "I realize it might not be easy to talk about, but—"

She cut him off. "He'll tell you everything. Everything. What he didn't tell the police. That's what you want to hear, isn't it?"

It took him a moment to respond to the unexpected question.

"Well?" she insisted.

"Yes," he said slowly. "Yes, that's what I want to hear. But why do you want to tell me?"

She looked, he thought, remarkably like a witch from a children's cartoon. White hair, slight hunch, long nose. She was quick like one, too.

Her words did nothing to alleviate the effect.

"Because you smell like them," she said.

The boy was back, handing Chris a glass of tepid water. He took it and tried to set it down, but there wasn't a clear surface in the room that he could see. "Um," he said. "Like who?"

She waved her hand dismissively. "You know who. Sonny, tell the man what you saw."

The boy fixed Chris's face with an intense expression—learned from his grandmother. "She disappeared," he said.

Chris sat up a bit straighter. "What? What do you mean? Who?"

"The woman who got shot," the boy said.

"After the killers left?"

"No, before. There was a light, all through the alley. It wrapped her up and she disappeared. And then they ran."

"And you didn't tell the police this?"

"Would you tell the police this?" the grandmother replied.

"Yes," Chris said. "I would. They deserve to know everything."

"They'd never believe it. They'd call his whole testimony into question, and then they'd send him off for counselling and he'd end up in a mental hospital."

Is that what happened to you? Chris wondered. He suspected the answer was yes. But she did have a point.

Although Lieutenant Jackson had seen enough at this point that, of everyone in the police department, he was probably most likely to accept a story about mysterious lights and disappearing bodies.

"I have always seen it," the grandmother said, as though she was making some grand announcement, "the other side. And no one has believed me. Now my grandson sees it too. You tell him what else you saw in that alley, Sonny."

Sonny straightened his skinny shoulders. "Demons."

Well. That was no great surprise.

"Could you describe any of the men?" Chris asked. "How many were there?"

"Three," Sonny said. "But it was too dark to see them. And they might have been wearing masks."

"Did you see a girl?" Chris asked, leaning forward. He set his tepid water on the floor. "About fourteen years old? Blonde? She's disappeared—the police think maybe the killers took her."

He shook his head. "Didn't see anybody like that. But I did see . . ." his voice dropped dramatically.

"Go on, go on," the grandmother said.

"She's not dead," the boy whispered.

Chris felt once again that the world was tipping to its side. Nothing about this visit was what he had expected.

"Who's not dead?"

"The woman they shot."

"That's impossible," Chris said.

"She was. But when the light came, it brought her back to life."

He sat back. "Wow."

The grandmother cackled. He could swear she'd stepped right out of a movie.

"Why are you telling me this?" Chris asked.

"I told you," the woman said. "I can smell them on you."

"Who are they?"

He asked, despite knowing the answer.

"The Oneness."

"I'm not one of them." He didn't know why he felt the need to assert that. There was something almost dangerous about this woman.

"I can see that. But they are chasing you down. Haunting you. The Spirit is haunting you. Yes?"

"I . . . I don't . . ."

She smiled, and something about her whole demeanour calmed. Suddenly Chris felt as though he was in a different place—like the cluttered, dark house had dimmed and been overtaken by another reality. And in this reality, the woman felt much less dangerous and much more like a friend.

"Who are you?" Chris asked.

"I am a witness."

"And your grandson . . ."

"Also a witness."

A shiver assailed him, despite the growing sense of safety in the atmosphere. "Not just of the murder."

"We are witnesses of many things."

"Can you tell me . . . what I've been seeing?" He explained to her about the child, and said, "I thought he must be part of the cloud. The dead."

She smiled. "The cloud are not dead; they are living, as you should know if you've seen them. But you are not correct in what you thought. No, what you are seeing is not of the cloud."

"A demon?"

"Not that either."

"What then?" His mind swept the possibilities—everything he'd learned about in the last short while. "An angel?"

"That is a more apt term. Though technically, an angel is one who bears a message. This being has given you no message?"

"He . . . it . . . doesn't seem to have much to say."

"Ah. I thought not. What you have seen is another being altogether. We call them Watchers."

Chris thought that one over. "Fine then. What is it . . . watching?"

"You, evidently."

"Why?" Chris asked. "I'm not even Oneness."

"Yet."

"This is supposed to be my choice."

"It is your choice."

"Then why do I feel like something's trying to force my hand?" He stood up so suddenly that he accidentally knocked his glass of water over. No one moved to clean it up. The grandmother and grandson were both still sitting, looking serenely—if intensely—up at him.

"You aren't human either, are you?" he said.

She smiled again. "Witnesses."

He thought about that. "Watchers."

She didn't answer.

He turned and blundered his way back out of the house, into the street and the sunlight. His heart was pounding out of his chest. He looked back, at the door hanging slightly ajar and the dark room beyond it.

"Learn anything?" Jackson asked. Chris jumped. He hadn't seen the lieutenant, who was leaning against the side of the house.

"No," Chris said.

Not anything he could repeat. Or explain.

And where the hell was Reese?

He just wanted to see her. Talk to her. Make sure she was okay. And maybe find his bearings again.

She had changed his life. If he didn't love her, he would hate her for it.

Jackson was looking at him skeptically. "Not sure I believe you. You look like you've seen a ghost."

He shook his head slightly. "Just an old lady. And her grandson."

"Yeah, I've met them."

"They strike you as odd?" Chris asked.

"No more than the usual recluse and her bully-targeted kid."

"Okay." Chris turned away from the house, surveying the street, looking up at the sky. He felt overcrowded by the houses and the caution tape and the whole dang city. He wanted to get back home, get out on the water, stand on the cliffs and stretch his soul out over the water.

"You sure they didn't tell you anything?"

Chris shook his head. "They're just . . . strange."

"Uh-huh." Jackson eyed him again. "You keep it to yourself, then. But I want to know when your girlfriend shows up."

Chris just nodded.

He wasn't sure what had just happened.

He had walked two blocks before he really realized that he was running away. He stopped and shook his head. The sky was clouding overhead, and it had grown colder. Likely there was a storm coming. He should have asked them more questions, he realized. The Witnesses. He should have asked them about Bertoller, and if they knew anything about what they had seen— about Julie's disappearance, the light, the men who had shot her.

The information they had given him hit him like a sack of concrete. He'd been so rattled by their strangeness that he hadn't really taken it in.

The boy said Julie had died and come back to life, and then disappeared.

So she was still . . . somewhere.

And Miranda hadn't been taken by the men. Which meant that Chris's own idea—that she had taken off on her own—was likely to be true. He needed to find her. Yes, he knew the police were looking, and that was good—but Chris had stayed in her home, and been part of tearing her world apart, and anyway, Reese cared about the girl and her mother. So he needed to help find her. A kid like that couldn't handle life on her own.

Especially not life in a world full of demons and who knew what else.

He turned to head back to the crime scene. He found Jackson easily.

"Where did you trace her phone call to?" he asked.

"Excuse me?"

"Reese. You said she called from a pay phone up north."

"Little logging town in the mountains," Jackson answered. "It's a three-day drive."

"When did she call?"

"Yesterday."

Disappointment coupled with determination filled him. "So she won't be here today. Can't make it back that fast. And she might not have gotten word right away."

"Most likely that's right," Jackson said. "No guarantees, though. She might have been headed back this direction already when she called. Why?"

"I want to help look for the kid," Chris said. "Just don't want to end up missing Reese."

"Look, we can find the kid if she's out there to be found."

"I think she is," Chris said. "Don't think she was kidnapped. I think she ran."

"Could be. We'll find her. You don't need to help."

"Yes, I do."

"Well, I can't stop you from looking. Just so long's you call me if you find her."

"That's it?" Chris asked. "You're not going to help me?"

"What do you want me to do, make you a deputy? Look,

I'm already in hot water for believing you people and giving you breaks. You want to look for the girl, look. But you're on your own."

"Yes, sir," Chris said. He scanned the street, like it would give him a clue.

And minutes later found himself knocking on the Witnesses' door again.

Once again it opened immediately, and two seconds later he was sitting on the love seat with another tepid water in his hand. He put it on the floor by the damp spot where the first one had spilled, placing his hands together.

"You said you didn't see a girl with the men who shot Julie," Chris said, addressing the boy. "Did you see a girl on her own?"

The grandmother cackled. "Oh, now he's asking the right questions."

The boy nodded. "Yes. She was scared. She ran away."

"When?"

"When the police came."

"Did she see the shooting and . . . and what happened after that?"

The boy shook his head. His hair was shaggy, like Tyler's. "Don't think so."

"But she must have known something had happened to Julie," Chris said half to himself. "Or she wouldn't have run."

"Maybe she went looking for her," the boy offered. "If she didn't see what happened, she might have thought her mother had left."

It was a thought. But where would she try to go?

Only one place Chris could think of.

He stood. "Thanks. You've been really helpful."

"Chris," the grandmother said. He looked down, ignoring the fact that she knew his name when he hadn't given it to her. She shook a long finger at him. "It's your choice. But don't wait forever to make it. Choices vanish when they're left alone too long."

"Thanks," he said, though he felt anything but thankful. He paused on his way out the door. "Anything else you didn't think to mention that you should have?"

They ignored the accusation. "You're not alone," the woman told him. "Whether you like it or not."

Those words were ringing in his ears as he jumped back into his truck and headed out of town.

He had no idea if Miranda would have made it back to the farm. Anything could have happened to her on the way there. But he was pretty sure that's where she would have tried to go. It was the only home she had, and the only place she would connect with her mother.

April stood at the kitchen table, leaning over Nick's shoulder and showing him how to shade in his sketch of a fishing trawler to give it greater depth. She talked as she worked, explaining each stroke.

"See?" she finished. She handed the graphite pencil back and flipped the page in his sketchbook to a drawing of a gull in the air. "Now your turn."

He started shading slowly, pausing after nearly every stroke to ask a question or receive encouragement. It was a beautiful day outside—sunny and crisp, with a sharply blue sky and calm water in the bay—but Nick had been indoors all morning and into the afternoon, drawing. Mary scolded him, but April interrupted and came to his defence. Yes, it was good for a boy to go outside. But it was good for the soul to draw.

He picked up speed as he gained confidence, and she stayed bent over the back of his chair, watching and commenting now and again until he finished.

"Well done," she said.

He looked up at her, blue eyes meeting blue eyes. "How about you?" he asked. "What are you drawing?"

She hesitated. Melissa entered the kitchen, a book in one hand and an empty tea cup in the other, which she set in the sink. The pianist paused by the sink and waited for April's answer.

"Not much," April said.

"Why?" Nick asked. "Don't you like to draw every day?"

"Well," April answered. "I did."

"Something changed?" Melissa asked.

"You might say that," April mumbled.

"You need to draw," Nick said. "It's important. Remember what you did in the cave."

"I haven't forgotten that," April said quietly.

Melissa regarded her curiously. April tried to laugh. "Okay, I'll draw something." She sat down and held her hand out. Nick pushed the sketchbook to her, and April picked up a pencil from Nick's collection, thought a moment, and sketched a quick caricature of Richard. She handed it back. Nick laughed.

"Happy now?"

"No," he said, although he was still grinning at the picture. "This isn't what you draw."

"I drew it," she pointed out. She sighed. "You're right, you're right. I will draw. I'm just taking a little break, you know? Speaking of which, you should take a break and go outside."

Nick pouted. "You told Mary to let me draw."

"And she did. Now you should go outside. It's a beautiful day. Get."

With exaggerated irritation, he stood up and started cleaning up his art supplies. She watched and smiled encouragingly at him as he headed upstairs to put them away.

Melissa moved to the table and sat down quietly. "So," she said, not meeting April's eyes, "why are you taking a break?"

"What happened in the cave . . ." April said. "Scares me."

"You nearly died there."

"Not that. The mural. The painting itself."

"It was that painting that brought me back to my senses," Melissa said. "That returned me to the Oneness. Nick's right. You need to draw."

April breathed out and looked down at her hands. "That's just it. That painting has done so much. It said so much. And more . . . it showed things, said things, that haven't happened yet. I feel responsible for it. And I'm not sure I can handle that responsibility."

"It was the Spirit that inspired the painting," Melissa said. "The Spirit's plan that poured through you. You are not responsible for that."

"But I am. You're an artist. You know. You're not just a tool. You're a creator. What you create comes from outside of you, maybe, but it goes through you, and you become part of it."

"A bit like life in the Oneness."

"I guess so."

She pushed back, away from the table. "I'm just scared. I can feel something building up inside me—like if I really started to draw or paint again, something would come out that's like the mural. And that scares me."

"I understand." April looked up and met Melissa's gaze. The pianist smiled. "I really do."

"So," April said, a mischievous smile coming to her face, "I haven't heard you play since you've been here. And we have a piano."

Melissa blushed. "I haven't wanted to intrude."

"Right," April said. "This is your home. And we're not actually a bunch of barbarians; I think we'd all love to hear you play."

"I'll make you a deal, then," Melissa said. "You bring a canvas down, and I will play while you paint."

"Hey now. That's not fair."

"I don't see why not."

April smiled. "All right then. Deal."

* * * * *

When Richard arrived from work, he walked into a house full of music, interspersed with low talking, laughter, and the smell of oil paints. Smiling, he peered into the long living room. Melissa sat at the piano, playing something simple but sweet, while a view of the bay from the top of the cliffs was appearing on April's canvas.

Without speaking, Richard sat on the leather couch and relaxed, listening with a smile on his face.

"Beautiful," he said when Melissa finished playing with a flourish. "Both of you."

Melissa turned on the piano bench and smiled at him, striking him to the heart. He didn't say any of the thousand things that crowded into his head. Instead, he looked at April's painting again. The familiar view shone in wet paint—the blue water and sky, both streaked with white, the long, pale grass at the top of the cliffs rimming it. He stood and came closer for a better look at it.

"Stunning," he said.

"Thank you," April said, a little shyly. Without the music accompanying it, the painting became the center of the room.

"Oh!" another voice said from the kitchen. Mary rushed in and came close to the painting, examining it. "Gorgeous."

"And innocent, thankfully," April said. She didn't explain what she meant, but Melissa stood and squeezed her arm.

"Oh, you're not getting up yet," Richard said. "You can't be done playing."

"Well . . ."

"Please?" Mary asked.

Melissa nodded and sat back down. The others arranged themselves around the room, and more drifted in—Shelley, Nick, Alicia, Diane. April sat down at first, but as the music filled the room—this time sweet but sad, deeply melancholy in its beauty—she stood again and went back to her canvas and brushes, adding detail while Melissa played.

When the song ended, it was as though the air was holding its breath. April stood still at her canvas, staring at it.

She had created something new.

No longer just an ocean scene.

Her hands began to tremble.

"April," Mary asked softly, joining her at the painting and laying her hand on her arm, "what is that?"

"I don't know," April whispered.

In the sky over the water April had painted light—like a sunrise in clouds, but the sky was cloudless and the light originated in itself and not in the sun. It spread itself across the clear blue with a subtle but potent force—a personality.

None of them had ever seen anything quite like it. Yet in the painting, it did not seem like something imagined.

"The ancients," Richard said, "used to describe something they called a bright cloud or cloud of light."

"What is it?" April asked.

But she didn't really need to—they all knew the answer.

The bright cloud was the Spirit made visible.

No one spoke the words; just left them hanging in the room.

"Why have you painted it?" Mary asked.

"I don't know. It just happened."

They stared at it in silence.

*   *   *   *   *

Rachel Starr Thomson

Even in the desert surroundings, the air was cool—autumn cool. Reese thanked the Spirit for that as she picked her way through the rolling, barren hills. In the distance the hills became foothills, and then mountains. She was angling herself away from them, trying to go southwest, toward where she thought—she hoped—the coast was. The closer she got to the ocean, the more likely she was to find a town or a highway.

She thought of Julie as she went. Julie, dead at the hands of Jacob's old enemy. Reese had been the one to bring Julie into the Oneness, and the connection formed between them in that moment had been strong—stronger than any tie natural to human existence. The strength of it was such that Reese found it incredibly hard to believe that Julie was dead. She could still feel her life, her essence, her energy, even though she must have passed into the cloud.

But the thought of that breach, of the split between heaven and earth, hurt.

And the idea of Julie being murdered—suffering whatever that had meant, enduring the violence to the soul of hatred and the violence to the body that was brutality—that hurt more.

She found herself wishing, fervently and half out loud, that Jacob had succeeded in killing Bertoller all those years ago. That he had not backed off, betrayed by his own tenderness. By the reticence to target any human being that was taught by the Oneness. She found herself wishing he had steeled his heart and his hands and just done the deed.

If he had, she wouldn't now be contemplating doing it herself.

It did have to be done. Of that she had become convinced.

Who would be next? Miranda? Lorrie, Jacob's wife? Or one of the village cell? Certainly they now numbered among Bertoller's chief enemies—prime targets. If they dispatched a hundred thousand demons, sent them screaming into the abyss, it wouldn't matter. The hatred was Bertoller's, and he would find a way to manifest it. He would always find a way to carry out what was in his heart.

Unconsciously, her sword formed in her hand. If the demons were there, they remained invisible—and she found that she didn't care.

More likely, the sword had formed in response to the thoughts in her heart.

As the hours passed, shadows shifted across the landscape, giving it a life of its own that Reese found eerie. Her sword remained in hand, like a reminder—but of what, she didn't know. She didn't bother to force it away. Being armed felt good out here.

Despite the cooler air, the sun's rays grew stronger as the approach of noon made them more direct. Reese found a twisted pine and sat beneath it, letting its branches provide shade. She didn't know how long she'd been walking . . . hours, judging from the sun.

Sitting forced her to face thoughts she'd been shoving aside with the action of hiking all morning. Contemplation on what exactly had happened when Tyler started to pray—and why she had fallen.

Especially on why she had fallen.

The first part was easy enough to guess at. He had wanted to tap into the Spirit in some way that would allow them to travel without the car—and faster. Somehow, he'd done it. The boy who had walked in the power of the Oneness had flown by the power of the Spirit.

She marveled at that. Maybe she'd been underestimating Tyler all this time. In a near lifetime of being Oneness, she had never seen anyone access the Spirit like that. Not ever.

But then again, maybe she had never seen anyone try.

It was the second part that bothered her more. She remembered the rush of wind and roar of flame that had lifted them out of the car—the physics of that, she wouldn't even try to figure out, nor what had happened to the car when they were somehow raptured out of it—and how startled—momentarily terrified, actually—she had felt. She remembered the sensation of flight, of being carried, and the world rushing by below, and then she remembered falling.

Why?

Vaguely she had a sense that something had pulled her down. If she tried, she thought she could remember—something clawing, tugging at her legs, pulling her off balance.

The same something that had caught her moments before she would have hit the ground?

The demon?

That made sense.

Except . . .

She groaned and buried her face in her hands. Why had a demon been able to reach her when she was caught up in the Spirit? How could it possibly have come so close?

Why, as she struggled to return to the light, did it seem she had been chosen by the darkness?

In the orchard, Tyler had suggested she pray. She hadn't done it. She'd said she wasn't much for prayer. And that was true. Reese had always found her points of communion with the Spirit in fellowship with the Oneness and in the rush of warfare.

Prayer was something more direct, more intimidating, and more demanding. Battle required discipline and a willingness to be wounded, but prayer required the disciplines of potential boredom, blind reaching, and a self-denial that went much deeper than withstanding pain. She had never been comfortable swimming in that particular ocean.

She ought to do it now. What else was there to do, lost in the desert?

She tried. She licked her lips and tried to verbalize something. Even to form a thought and send it in the Spirit's direction.

Nothing came.

Instead, she rose and kept on going through the dry hills.

As the sun crested the top of the sky and began its way down again, Reese became aware of two things: that she was incredibly thirsty, and that something was tracking her.

The hunters were back.

She turned and glared at the landscape behind her, not bothering to hide that she knew they were there. She could see nothing.

But every instinct told her something was there.

Picking up her pace, she started to trace a more erratic route across the desert, following shadows and heading for a region with more scrub and rock—more cover. She was alone, and if she was going to be in a fight, she needed something at her back.

A rocky outcrop covered on three sides with scrub, crowned by scraggly pines, and faced with sheer rock on one side was perfect. She made her way toward it, finding that she was glad for this—itching for it, actually. She needed a fight. She needed to take out her confusion and aggression and anger on someone. She needed an enemy with a face.

She wasn't expecting the face that presented itself.

The bear in the woods, the one that had spoken with Jacob's voice and had a man's face, had looked like a stranger.

The creature that approached her now, ethereal, pulled together as from cloud and not from flesh at all, wore the face of David.

* * * * *

Chris parked his truck in front of the farmhouse and got out, breathing in the cool air. The season had changed from stifling heat to the cool of fall overnight. He welcomed the relief. It was bracing—just what he needed, given everything he was facing. Some of the leaves in the trees around the farm were already going gold and brown, as though they'd anticipated the change in the weather before it came. Responding to cues no one else could see or feel.

His approach to the house scattered chickens, which were ranging free in the yard and clucking loudly, and set a dog to barking. The animal came bounding from the back of the house, a black lab mix, wagging its tail. Chris held out his hand, let the dog sniff it, making friends quickly. The lack of human response to his presence was eerie. A tractor sat abandoned in the field next to the house; the barn doors stood open. No one had been here since the death and subsequent arrests. The farmhouse stood lonely.

Chris approached it slowly, eyes and ears open for any sign of Miranda. When she didn't appear, he stepped onto the porch and knocked at the front door. He waited several minutes before knocking again, and then calling out, "Miranda? It's Chris. Are you here?"

He was kicking himself, telling himself he'd been wrong and followed a false trail, when the door cracked open.

Miranda's wide blue eyes peered out.

"Hey," Chris said. "Are you going to let me in?"

Without a word, she opened the door all the way.

"Thanks." He had barely stepped inside when she threw herself into his arms and burst into tears, her sobs getting louder and less controlled by the moment.

"It's okay," he said, stroking her hair and letting her cling to him. "It's all right. I just came to check on you. What are you doing here?"

His calm tone pushed her away from hysteria, and she managed to gasp out an answer. "I just . . . came . . . to look for . . . my mother."

"Yeah, that's what I thought," Chris said. Gently, he pried her arms loose and steered her toward a flowered couch in the living room. "Sit," he said. "And tell me why you thought she would be here."

"She disappeared," Miranda said, holding her hands together so tightly her knuckles turned white. "She left the safe house. She said she wouldn't leave me!"

"I don't think she meant to," Chris said. "But take it easy . . . why did you think she would come here?"

"Because she said she wanted to. They think she killed that man, and she thought if she could come back here she could find some proof that she didn't. But she said she wouldn't leave me, and she's not here, and . . ."

"I think she's okay," Chris said. He knelt down, took her arms, and looked her firmly in the eye. "Miranda, listen. Don't panic at what I'm going to tell you. The police think your mother has been killed. You might even hear that on the news. But I believe she's all right. I met a witness who says she's okay."

"Where is she?" Miranda asked, a note of panic coming into her voice despite Chris's admonitions.

"I don't know," he said, "but I'm going to take care of you until we find her, or she finds us. Okay?"

"O . . . kay. Where's Reese?"

He winced. "I don't know that either. But I think she's going to come looking for your mom, and then we can connect with her too. She'll help look after you."

He didn't tell her that Jacob was most likely with Reese. He suspected that would trigger Miranda's always-latent hysteria, and that just wouldn't do anyone any good. She seemed to have steadied out for the moment.

"How long have you been here?" he asked. "And how did you get here?"

"I hitchhiked," Miranda said. "Last night."

"Don't do that again," Chris said, a little sharply.

"I got here."

"It's not safe. Especially not for someone like you."

"Fine," she said, folding her arms and huddling back into the couch. Pouting. The girl was fourteen at least, but she looked for all the world like a small child.

"So what have you done since you've been here?"

"Just looked for Mom, and then changed my clothes and took care of the chickens. There's a lot of work to do around here. The police should let some of our people go so they can come back and take care of the animals."

Unlikely, Chris thought, given that there had been another murder in connection with the community. At least, everyone thought there had. He thought over Sonny's words—his confident assertion that Julie had indeed been shot but then had come back to life and been spirited away.

Spirit. Whatever exactly that word meant, it was changing Chris's world in ways he found incredibly unsettling.

"That your dog outside?" he asked.

"That's Testy. He's Jacob's dog."

"He's pretty friendly."

"Yeah. He's supposed to be a guard dog, but he's no good at it."

As if on cue, Testy started barking. Chris moved to the window and looked out.

"Miranda," he said, "do you know someone who drives a black Cadillac?"

"No . . ."

The dog was growling now, and menacing the car and its inhabitants.

"Go upstairs," Chris said. "Hide."

"What? Why?"

"Stay calm," he commanded, responding to the rising pitch of her voice. "Just do what I tell you. Now!"

Whimpering, Miranda jumped off the couch and ran for the stairs. Chris stayed by the window, standing out of sight where he could see out but no one could see him.

Testy was backing away from the car, still barking but evidently unwilling to attack the men emerging from the car. There were four of them. All four wore black suits and carried handguns.

"Not exactly the friendly neighbour type, are you?" Chris said in a low voice.

Testy continued to circle the men, trying to hold them at bay with his barking and growling but not actually attacking them. They mostly ignored him and advanced on the house.

Chris regretted having sent Miranda upstairs. He should have told her to find a back door and get out.

He should do the same, but he couldn't leave the house with her still in it.

Cursing under his breath, he sprinted to the stairs as the men pounded on the front door. He didn't think they were going to take "no answer" as a reason to leave. Positioning himself near the top of the staircase, he listened for their further progress. In a moment he heard the front door open—he should have locked it—and the men enter.

"Search it," one of them said. "Find the woman."

They were looking for Julie too.

So Sonny was right—she had disappeared.

The staircase ended in a blind corner, and Chris moved around it so he could hear anyone coming up before they could see him. The open door at the bottom of the stairs made it more likely they would come up soon, but it also allowed him to hear what was going on below—a fair trade.

For a split second he thought he saw his child Watcher friend sitting on the bottom step.

At least he wasn't alone.

Standing with his back to the wall, he scanned the hallway for something he could use as a weapon or for any sign of what room Miranda had gone into. All the bedroom doors were closed, and the hallway was mostly clear of clutter. A small, narrow hall table stood against one wall, sporting a doily and a decorative vase. Chris picked the vase up but discarded it as too light to be any use, then picked up the table itself. He could use it as a club or a shield, as necessary.

From the sounds downstairs, the men had fanned out into other parts of the first floor. Chris took the opportunity to open the bedroom door he was most familiar with—the door to the room where he had stayed during his and Tyler's short imprisonment here. A hall table wasn't going to do much good against guns, especially once the whole group was alerted to his presence; better to keep retreating as long as he could.

If only he knew where Miranda was.

He measured the wisdom of searching for her—equally afraid of making noise that would attract attention from the thugs downstairs and growing too distracted in his search to notice them coming up—and was spared from making a decision when her frightened whisper met his ears from the closet in the room.

"Chris?"

"Good," he said quietly. "Good that you're here. Stay quiet."

He scanned the room and noted the oak tree outside the window. It would take a little courage, but it should be possible for both of them to climb across the slight roof outside the window and then jump into the tree, and from there to reach the ground.

Of course, they took a risk of being seen.

Voices and footsteps on the stairs decided it for him. He quietly closed the bedroom door, shoved the hall table under its handle, and pulled Miranda out of the closet with his finger on his lips.

"We're going out the window," he whispered.

"I can't!"

"Yes, you can. And you can do it quietly. You have to. Just trust me."

She whimpered as he steered her across the room and opened the window. It was an easy climb to the roof, if slightly nerve-racking—the shingled surface was steeply pitched. Her whimpering was growing to a whine. He shushed her sternly, and she silenced herself, her face white.

He opted to go first. The last thing he needed was Miranda falling off the roof, and it would be easier to get her to climb down to him then to convince her to get out there alone. He swung himself down easily and reached up for her with one hand while he gripped the windowsill with the other.

"Come on," he whispered. "Easy does it."

Her long dress made the climb awkward, but she half-climbed, half-toppled out of the window, and he set her feet firmly on the roof.

Below them in the yard, Testy appeared. He barked once and paced below them, wagging his tail.

Chris surveyed the jump. A strong, gnarled branch swept out just past the roof. All Miranda needed to do was jump to it and then hand-over-hand her way to the tree so she could climb down. It should be plenty strong enough to hold them both.

In his mind's eye, the men were all the way upstairs and were going through the bedrooms. They might come in at any moment and see the open window and hear the rustling in the tree as they made the leap.

No time to waste.

"See that branch?" Chris said, pointing. "Jump to it and grab it and then get yourself over to the tree trunk."

"I can't!" She was too loud—almost wailing.

"Hush," he insisted. "You can, and you're going to. I'll be right behind you."

She backed up, pressing herself against the house and pulled herself away from Chris's arm. "I can't."

He considered throwing her. And imagined the result if she just panicked and let herself fall.

"You have to do this!" he stage-whispered. "We don't have time. Trust me."

She shook her head, plastering herself even tighter against the house.

Chris was about to grab her and throw her after all when Testy started barking wildly and a man walked around the outside of the house.

One of the intruders.

The man glared at the dog and cursed it. Miranda whimpered again, and Chris realized he had grabbed her arm and was squeezing it far too hard. He loosened his grip and tried to communicate calm and control. They had moved over enough to be clear of the window, but it was still open—if the man on the ground looked up, or if the intruders came into the bedroom and checked out the roof, they would be caught.

He allowed himself to hope that the intruders didn't really expect to find anyone and so wouldn't look out the open window.

Considering that they had bothered to come out here in the first place, the hope was slight at best.

Testy had lowered himself into a crouching, growling stance, and he circled the man with evident threat. The intruder cursed again, and took a step closer to the house.

The dog charged. Miranda screamed.

Chris clapped a hand over her mouth, his heart pounding as the sound of a shot reverberated in his ears.

The shot had covered the sound of her scream. He hoped.

Tears were filling Miranda's eyes, but the dog seemed unharmed—he had yelped and moved back a distance, but it looked like the shot had missed. The gunman cursed again, yelled something in a language that wasn't English, and disappeared around the other side of the house again. In a moment other voices, all speaking whatever the other language was, shouted at him. Chris closed his eyes as the men argued with each other.

And he heard footsteps in the bedroom.

Leaving.

Moments later they both heard a car starting up and driving away.

Good dog, Chris thought.

He couldn't bring himself to speak out loud.

That evening, April borrowed Richard's car without asking and headed up the coast toward Tempter's Mountain. She didn't tell anyone where she was going.

She needed to revisit the death cave, and she wanted to do it alone.

Weeks had passed since her imprisonment and near-starvation there. Weeks during which she had concentrated on healing and trying to get her bearings back. But the cave had not vanished into memory. It had taken on life of its own, the prophecies painted across its walls not only being fulfilled, but playing an active role in their own fulfilment by opening eyes and prompting action. Prophecies she had painted. Without having any idea what she was doing.

Teresa, the cloud member who had visited her in the cave, had told her that she had great significance and that we do not know who we ourselves are. Richard had told her, after the rescue, that he believed her to be one of the great saints.

A term which, even now, made her want to laugh incredulously. She was not great. She was simply April. Oneness with a troubled past and a propensity to draw and paint and run. The only "great" thing she had done in her entire life was snatching Nick out from under the nose of the hive. And even that wasn't much—she'd just been in the right place at the right time.

Except for the mural in the death cave. That seemed like something a great saint would create.

As did the painting she'd done today. She had painted the Spirit—in visible form.

She had never heard of anyone doing that before.

The road looped along the coast, through yellow sand bluffs and pine stands. The blue water to her left shone in the lowering evening sun. She was glad for the beauty and for the vast expanse—they allowed her to consider all these things without folding in too tightly upon herself. To remember that all that happened to her happened in a wider world of purpose. It was good to have that assurance, because April was not sure who she was anymore, and the need to know would be crippling if she didn't think the answer existed out in that wider world—if the Spirit didn't have a plan.

She was hoping the cave could help. She remembered very little about her time there—being hit on the head before David's thugs dumped her there probably had something to do with that. She could barely remember doing the painting or what it looked like. Her clearest memories, in fact, were of Teresa's presence. So she hoped that getting back to the cave would bring something back; would help her remember what had happened and how she had managed to paint detailed prophecy of the calibre that she had. Maybe if she could remember that, she could understand something more about who and what she was.

She left the water behind as she turned up the back roads to Tempter's Mountain, bouncing through unkempt territory until she parked in front of the hermit's little cottage. It was empty, of course, and silent. Monument to a life that had crossed over into a greater reality.

She wasn't exactly sure how to find the death cave, but she'd managed to weasel general directions out of Richard without telling him why she wanted them. Without stopping to look in on the cottage, she headed up the paths behind it that led down the cliffs.

She felt the cave before she saw it—felt it as a growing edginess, a knot in her gut. She wasn't surprised to feel it, or to sense it turning into fear. She had nearly died here, after all. Nearly been killed by a cruel enemy.

That was another reason she needed to know who she was. If she was someone worth murdering, she wanted to know why.

The path was steep and littered with stones and roots, and she made her way carefully down it, ignoring the growing impulse to turn and run. When the entrance came in view, a dark blot on the cliff side, she forced one foot in front of the other until she reached the opening.

It smelled rank. She stepped in and flipped on the flashlight in her hand before she could lose her nerve, passing the iron door into the depths of the prison in the cliff. She swept the walls with light.

And went cold.

The mural was there—but defaced. Deep black gouges like claw marks raked across it, and someone had altered the pictures themselves with grotesque imagery in black.

In the center of the mural was a new picture—one she had not drawn. She recognized it, of course—it was the face that looked back at her from any mirror. But her face was twisted as though in torment.

Written over it letters gouged out of the rock were the words,

FOUND YOU.

She turned, very slowly.

Something was standing behind her.

*   *   *   *   *

Chris waited until the car had been gone twenty minutes before he released Miranda's arm and said, "Okay. We can get down. I'll go first and pull you up." She nodded, her face tear-streaked. She had cried the entire time, but at least had done it silently.

He climbed back through the window and noted signs that someone had searched the room—the intruder must have been there when the gun went off, which was why Chris hadn't heard him come in. He imagined the man looking out the window to see where the shot had come from. With his eyes drawn to the dog and the man below, he must not have looked to the side where Chris and Miranda were standing only inches away.

So many things could have gone wrong. He could have

yelled at his compatriot, drawing the attention of the man on the ground to the window and the roof. Miranda could have screamed again, or made any sound loud enough to draw either man's attention. They could have decided to move at exactly the wrong time.

"Thank you," he told no one as he turned around to pull Miranda up.

He did not know who he was talking to, but he was certain that someone had heard.

"I'm getting as weird as Tyler," he muttered.

"What?" Miranda asked, clinging to his arm with both hands as he hauled her off the roof and back through the window.

"Nothing." He set her on the floor and looked at her sternly. "Okay," he said, "we survived that. But there are two things we need to learn from this. First, that we might have someone after us, and we need to be careful. Second, that you need to learn to be quiet."

She burst into tears again, but thankfully didn't wail. "I'm sorry . . . I couldn't help it! I was just so scared. And I thought he was going to shoot Testy . . ."

"He might have shot us if he'd found us. Or worse. Look, I don't want to scare you, but if I'm going to take care of you, then I need you to help me do it. And that means no hysterics when I need you to be brave."

He knelt and looked her in the eye, struck again by how young she seemed—by how much he felt like he was talking to a child and not a young woman. "You can do that," he said. "Your mother is a brave woman, and from now on, so are you."

"Are we going to find my mother?" Miranda asked, her voice wobbly. But she dashed her tears away, and none came to replace them.

"Yes, we are," Chris said. "Somehow."

"Both of us?"

"Both of us. Because you are going to be brave."

She nodded. "I'll try."

He smiled. "Good. Now that that is settled, you can help me think. This was your home. Do you know anywhere else that your mother would have gone? Or anywhere people are likely to look for her?"

Miranda shook her head.

"Do you have family somewhere?"

Miranda shrugged, looking sorrowful. "Just the community. And they're all in jail or in custody like we were."

"Your mother didn't have anyone else? Parents, sisters and brothers?"

"Nobody I knew," Miranda said. "We moved here when I was born, and Mama said we left our old life behind forever."

Chris wondered if Julie was regretting that decision right about now. He wanted to push harder, but remembering that Miranda hadn't known her own address when she first called the village cell to tell them about the death, he figured it wouldn't do much good.

"Did Jacob keep records on the community anywhere?" he asked. "Important papers, letters, anything?"

At that, Miranda brightened. "He kept letters sometimes—

in his office. When mail would come sometimes he said it was better if we didn't read it."

Chris thought angry things but said nothing. Might as well not stir Miranda up anymore than she already was. She bolted off in the direction of the stairs. "Come on, I'll show you where it is!"

"Hey, don't be so loud!" he called out after her as she clattered down the stairs, he catching up as quickly as he could. She waited at the bottom.

"There's no one here."

"They could always come back. Just keep it down."

Miranda led Chris out of the house to one of the barns in back that had several extra rooms built into one end. Jacob's office was central—and padlocked.

"Great," he said. "Do you know where there's a key?"

"No," Miranda said, "but we can shoot it off. I know where there's guns."

Not only did she know where there were guns—unguarded and easy to access—she also knew how to shoot them. Chris watched with a mixture of amusement and alarm as she shot the padlock off the door with easy confidence.

"Well," he said. "Thanks."

He pushed open the door and entered a neat, practical room with little decoration. Bookshelves lined two walls, laden with thick tomes—a mix of theology, practical manuals, and other things Chris didn't take the time to figure out—and a large, handmade wooden desk sat against another. A collection of saws of different types and sizes hung on the wall, the only attempt at decorating. But it was the filing cabinets on the fourth wall, on both sides of the door, that interested Chris most.

"He kept all of that stuff here?" he asked, pointing to the cabinets.

Miranda shrugged. "I guess so. This is where he took most anything."

The cabinets were unlabelled—and locked. The shotgun would be little help this time, since Chris didn't want any of the files to end up casualties. He started hunting around for a key while Miranda watched.

"You going to give me a hand?" he asked, looking up from the desk drawers where he was rooting through pens, staplers, and other desk clutter.

"Don't think he kept the keys in here," she said. "He always wore a bunch of keys around his neck. Probably that's where they are."

"Well, that doesn't help us now." Chris shut the desk drawer and paused, leaning on the desk surface with one hand while he tried to think of another way into the cabinets. His eyes raised to the saws. "Ah," he said. "I think I found our way in."

Ten minutes and a fight with a noisy electric saw later, he had taken the locks off a cabinet and was going through the first drawer. Bills. The second drawer yielded warranties for much of the equipment around the farm. It wasn't until the third drawer that he found something that interested him.

"Here we go," he said, taking out a manila folder with a name on it. Miranda, perched on the desk looking bored to death, perked up.

"What's that say?" she asked.

"Christopher Hawkins," he answered.

"That's one of the men who lived here."

Chris flipped the file open and started riffling through the papers. Yes, this was what he wanted—life insurance papers, birth certificate, other ID, more. He stuck the file back in and went through the others until he came to one marked "Julie Hunter."

The chances that this file would lead to her might not be high, but right now it was the only thing he had to go on.

The file was thick, and he saw why as soon as he opened it—it was full of unopened mail. They were all postmarked from the same place, with the same name on the return address.

"Who is Andrew Hunter?" he asked. He only heard Miranda's answer with half his brain—the other half was absorbed in the answer, which he discovered in the next piece of paper. A marriage certificate, dated sixteen years ago, for Andrew and Julie Hunter.

"Oh," he said. He looked up at Miranda. "What did you say?"

"I said I don't know," Miranda said.

He cleared his throat. "Did your mom ever talk to you about your father?"

"He died before I was born," Miranda said.

Chris looked back down at the sheaf of unopened mail in his hands. The last postmark was two years ago.

Had Julie known about these? Or was Jacob keeping them from her?

He decided against telling Miranda.

"Does that file say something about him?" she asked, curiosity itself.

"There's a marriage certificate," Chris said. "For your parents."

He flipped through a little more—life insurance. One beneficiary: Jacob. Various forms of ID. More mail—this time with a return address Chris recognized as Julie's parents. They were several states away. Would she go to them?

Or to her husband?

"Who told you about your father's death?" Chris asked, slowly.

"Jacob did."

He looked up. "Not your mom?"

"She doesn't like to talk about him."

"So Jacob told you . . ."

"That my dad died before I was born. Why do you want to know this, anyway?"

He looked back down at the papers. If Julie knew her husband was still alive, and if she had any idea that he'd been trying to contact her for years, maybe she would go to him now. That seemed the most natural thing to do.

But then again, Julie had been living in a cult for fifteen years. And now, thanks to Reese, she was Oneness. Who knew what she would do? Oneness wasn't natural. In all kinds of ways.

Frustrated, he closed the file and tucked it under his arm. It was a place to start. For now, he wanted to get off this property. "Come on," he said. "We're going."

She hopped off the desk. "Where?"

"I'm not sure yet. But I've got a couple of ideas."

She followed him out the door—and they both stopped short.

"Put your hands up," the man in black said, pointing a gun at them.

The other three men stood behind him, smirking.

They had come back.

April steeled herself as she turned. Faint light outlined the silhouettes of an old, hunched man and a cadre of others, all dressed in black. She could see none of their faces, but she could clearly feel the menace in their presence.

She knew who the old man was—the only person it could be. "Clint" was back.

"I thought we would find you here," he said. "Dogs always return to their vomit. Patience pays off."

"What do you want?" April asked.

The old man waved his hand, taking in the mural. "You thought you controlled the future. But you see, we can also make our mark. You can do nothing we cannot deface. Assert yourself, and we will always be there to bring you down."

"What do you want with me?" she asked again.

"Your life," he said. "The same thing we wanted last time. But as it turns out, your escape works in my favour. I need power now. Your friends took it from me. And you are going to give it back."

"I won't help you," April said.

"You don't have any choice."

"You can't force my help," she said.

"In fact, we can. Because all I need you to do is die. And you will find you cannot prevent that."

April closed her eyes as two of the black-clothed men took her roughly by the arms. There was no point in fighting them, not here—she was as thoroughly trapped as it was possible to be.

I should have told someone where I was going, she thought as the men shoved her forward.

Outside the cave, blocking the path back to the hermit's cottage, a creature stood—half again the height of a man, hunched, and dark in colour. April tried to take in its features but found she couldn't look directly at it—like a shadow, it shifted. She could make out massive claws, the defacers of the cave.

The old man led them along another path, going south along the edge of the sea. It angled sharply upward and moved out onto a sheer cliff hundreds of feet above the water. Gulls and other sea birds dashed out from nests in the cliff face, circling and calling and then coming home. It was a dizzying sight.

Dizzying, blue, and free.

It only took April an instant to decide. Her captors' grip had loosened on her arms as they toiled up the steep path.

She wrenched herself free of them and threw herself over the cliff.

* * * * *

Melissa was stepping over the kitchen threshold when something washed over her so strongly that she stumbled and fell nearly to her knees with a cry. Richard dashed to her side, catching her arm and stopping her fall, as Mary came to her other side—

And Melissa called out, "April!"

April's name hammered through her heart as a vision of blue sky and water blotted out her view of the house. She could feel spray and wind sucking the air out of her lungs. She reached out, feeling Mary and Richard on either side of her like an extension of her reach, all three of them forming a net—

And she came back to the room. Richard and Mary lowered her to the floor as she fought to catch her breath.

"What just happened?" she asked.

"I don't know," Richard said. "What did you—"

"April . . . something about April. I saw sky and water. And felt like I was . . . falling?"

"Where is April?" Mary asked. "Richard?"

"I thought she was here." His words hung in the air for a moment before he dashed away, and Mary sat with Melissa, rubbing her shoulders and offering silent comfort, while they listened to him searching. He was back in minutes.

"She's gone. And so is my car."

"She didn't tell you where she was going?" Mary asked.

"If she had, we wouldn't be having this conversation. Melissa, tell us exactly what you saw."

"I—" she stopped and thought. "I didn't see April, but I felt her. Like her name was just in my heartbeat all of a sudden. It hit me like a weight. And then I saw blue—sky and ocean. It felt like all the air was being sucked out of my lungs."

"You reached out," Richard said. "To catch her?"

Melissa thought about it. Everything had been so instinctive, she hadn't thought about what she was doing in those terms. "Yes? That makes sense."

"April, where are you?" Richard asked.

But no one expected an answer.

* * * * *

"Get down there now!" Bertoller shrieked, his eyes riveted on the water where his prize had disappeared. "Find her!"

The creature had already begun to vault down the cliff face, its claws giving it a way down where there was no path. But Bertoller had no interest in trusting April to the beast. It would likely find her first; his men needed to be there to stop it from ripping her throat out prematurely. Damned bloodhound.

"She won't have survived that fall," one of his men offered, nervously.

"Don't you tell me what she won't have survived," Bertoller spat. "Fool. She's a fool. Get down there, I tell you. I don't want the beast to find her and kill her before I have my way."

"But sir—"

"She's a great saint," Bertoller said, tearing his eyes away from the water and fixing them on his lackey. "Do you know what that means?"

"I . . . no, sir."

"Then shut your mouth and do what I tell you. She's survived. Find her, take her, and don't let the beast kill her. Understood?"

The man saluted. "Sir." He turned and started barking orders, the men picking their way around the cliff in search of a way down. Bertoller restrained himself from picking them up and pitching them over the side. Much as he wanted to, he knew his men wouldn't survive the fall—and he needed every last one of them, thanks to the ripping away of his powers he had suffered at the hands of those insolent thieves.

The Oneness. How he hated them—how he longed to tear every last one of them limb from limb, to tear them from each other, to rip them out of the heart of the Spirit and cast them into the chaos that answered to his call.

For now, he would settle for recapturing the girl and killing her properly. He grimaced—the closest he could come to a smile—at the thought of how the others would react. Of how her death would hurt them, tear at them. It might even finally turn the girl called Reese, if he could only find a way to make her feel responsible for it.

That shouldn't be too hard. The girl was keeping company with Jacob. She already carried enough guilt to destroy her. He just needed to unleash it.

Franz Bertoller's hatred of the Oneness went deep, far, and hundreds of years back. He had battled them for centuries before realizing that simply fighting them did no good. That if he truly wanted to inflict damage, he would do it by infiltrating their ranks and turning their hearts. He would do it with guilt, and condemnation, and hatred, and fear, and greed. Everything that had kept the rest of the world locked in the destructive patterns of warmongering for millennia. The Oneness might be well shielded against all of those things, but they were not immune. He had proven that with David and Jacob and nearly the woman called Melissa. And Reese had almost gone down with them all.

She would still, he promised himself. When he finished destroying Jacob, Reese would be there to unravel with him.

April had been the wild card, the one who stood in the way of success. The Power had told him that she was a great saint, though unaware and not yet unleashed. He could not wage his war while she had a chance of rising. So he had sent his men to kill her before she could take her place. Cowards, they had left her to starve instead—and she'd been rescued.

But it was all for the best after all. Stripped of his powers, Bertoller needed something truly grandiose to get them back. Sacrificing a great saint to the Power would suffice.

He growled. His men had not yet found a path down.

He could not afford to lose her again.

* * * * *

April hit the water and plunged into the cold, salty world

beneath with more awareness than she expected—somehow she'd thought she wouldn't hit conscious. But a moment before her body hit the surface she felt as though arms came beneath her and caught her up, buoying her just enough to break the fall and lower her into the water gently.

Gently, she thought as she sank, and laughed underwater.

She'd thought to die when she threw herself off that cliff— just to do it in some way that would thwart the old man.

She hadn't thought to be caught, to live, to experience the unexpected beneath the waves.

But as she continued to sink, straight down like a diver rather than buoying up again, she found herself following a purpose she hadn't known about it until now; answering a call—

Something was drawing her down here.

She had cast herself off the cliff because she heard it calling.

She remembered that now. She could feel the aftereffects of the voice, like an echo, too faint to make out the words but undeniably there. It had summoned, and without consciously hearing the summons she had answered it.

Still she was sinking—diving down, watching the water world pass in patterns of light and darkness, the way surprisingly clear before her. No fish, no fronds, nothing but water and light and shadow.

And before her, below her, shadows that were darker and deeper still.

She was aware of pressure growing as she dove ever deeper, but not of pain nor of panic.

She did not need to breathe, she realized.

It wasn't as though she was breathing. She simply didn't need to.

Her surroundings washed black, and then darker even than black.

She hadn't known the ocean was so deep here. She thought the bay was shallow . . . certainly this close the cliffs.

But she was not close to the cliffs.

She knew that in the same way she remembered the voice summoning her. It was an echo, something someone had told her and she had forgotten.

And then, below her, she saw a light.

Just a pinprick at first, then growing. White light. And now it was pulsing, slowly, like a thing alive.

And she was suspended somewhere in the deep darkness, upright (she thought), still not needing to breathe. The water was not cold; if anything, it was overly warm. And the light reached out like filaments in the dark and wrapped itself around her, One-ing itself with her until she could see it glowing from her fingers and hands and feet and the strands of her hair that floated in front of her face.

Where am I? she asked, though she did not open her mouth.

In the deep places of the earth, a voice answered. She heard it clearly this time, in the present—not as a faint memory from the past, though it was that too. Now that she heard it so clearly, she knew she had heard it a thousand times before. It had spoken through the Oneness, and even before then—she had known it as a child.

The deep places . . . April answered.

You have been here before.

I would remember.

You do remember.

Oh . . . yes. All at once, she did.

You tell me, the voice said. Where are you, Child of Light?

In the womb, she answered. But I don't understand how that can be.

In the beginning, the voice said, the earth was without form, and void, and it was swaddled in the waters. Like every human being created in the womb of its mother—the soul is a universe brought forth from the darkness where I knit it together. In the dark place—the deep place.

Where you . . .

Yes.

April turned herself slowly, searching the shadows for a form, somewhere she could locate the presence that spoke. But there was nothing, and even as she tried to see, she knew she was looking in the wrong way. That the darkness itself was the form of this being, that these shadows were alive.

I thought darkness belonged to the enemy, she said.

Nothing belongs to the enemy.

Is this darkness you? Is this what you look like?

No. The darkness shrouds—conceals. As the womb conceals the life being formed in it and the waters conceal the earth.

Then what do you look like?

There was a smile to the dark.

Must you ask that, Child of Light?

She thought again, letting time pass—if time had meaning here. The voice seemed in no hurry.

This . . . deep place. This is a womb?

This is the womb, the voice answered.

Then something is being birthed here.

Being formed. Before the time of birthing comes.

What something?

The smile again.

What is here? she asked, and then thought, I am.

And so am I.

You are the Spirit.

Of course.

She could think of nothing else to say, but: I didn't know.

April awoke on the sand.

She was wet, soaked through, but nothing hurt, and her breathing was relaxed and regular—no water in her lungs, no desperate need for air. Birds were circling overhead and the air smelled like wet sand and fish and salt water.

A dark shadow lurched above her field of vision, and she slowly drew herself up and backed away, toward the water, trying to take in the sight. It was the beast from the cavern, throwing itself down the cliff from landing place to landing place as fast as it could. They were after her.

But beyond the creature, and the men she could just make out coming down a path some distance away, the cliff itself and the sky and the sun and the water in her peripheral vision was pulsating with light.

The light she had painted while Melissa played.

The light that was the answer to her question in the deep place—"What do you look like?"

And she smiled up at it, welcoming it, laughing into its golden reality.

What else could she do?

The beast was close. Checking on the whereabouts of all her pursuers again, she made a fervent wish that none of them had spotted her and turned and dove into the bay, holding her breath and swimming underwater.

Light from above sparkled off her skin as she swam—and light from within radiated from it.

Reese stood frozen against the rock face, sword in hand, staring at the apparition as it drew closer across the desert floor. It was a hundred yards away now, passing through cloud shadows and seeming to lose itself in them, only to re-form when it stepped back into the sun. Its eyes were fixed on her—it seemed not to need to look at the ground.

The sight of the ghost sucked all the fight from her lungs. She couldn't battle this.

Could she?

As it came nearer, she lifted her voice and called, "You aren't dead?"

It couldn't really be him—couldn't be David, dead and part of the cloud. A demon in the form of her worst enemy she could face, but she couldn't stand an encounter with the man himself.

The cell had been right not to assign her to him. To send

her after Jacob, make her remove herself far from the man who had exiled her.

The man who had watched her friend die with a smile.

The man who had torn her spirit apart.

He did not answer.

She closed her eyes for a moment, hoping frantically to find something inside her that would tell her the truth. She found it, in the form of her sword hilt—more solid and heavy in her hand than she had ever felt it. It would not so form itself in the presence of Oneness.

Even if she hated the one connected to her.

When she opened her eyes again, its feet were drifting away, like smoke being blown in the wind. It seemed to struggle to hold itself together. No wonder, really—there could be nothing in this barren region to fuel it, to give it power to take form. This was not the warehouse.

It would have been far easier to find some desert creature to possess. So the demon meant something by this—this was strategy.

Strategy for a different sort of fight.

Reese drew a deep breath and let her sword dissolve.

"What do you want?" she asked.

The demon drew level with her and looked into her eyes with its unnervingly familiar ones—with the face of a man who had been like a father to Reese for most of her life.

"I should ask you that," it said.

"What do you mean?"

"You called me here."

Reese jerked back as if she'd been slapped. "I didn't. You've been tracking me."

"I have been answering to your summons."

"That's impossible."

"Is it?" The familiar face smiled, and David's voice lapsed into tones Reese knew as well as her own—ironic, comforting, convincing. "We've been here every time you've needed us. You've been searching for answers. We have them. You fell, we caught you. You think that's all coincidence?"

"Why are you . . ." she choked, and kept going. "Why are you wearing David's face?"

"Because you want to face him."

"I don't understand."

"Don't you?"

And she did . . . that was the problem. She did understand. She knew the creature was right. She had been calling to them, wanting what they had to offer. All but asking for their help. Not consciously . . .

But not entirely unconsciously either.

"Where is David?" she asked the demon.

"In jail. Awaiting trial."

"Do you know how the trial will go?"

"We have looked into the future, yes."

"And?"

"He's found a good lawyer . . . Bertoller has paid for one. Most of the men who could have testified against him are dead or clearly insane. He'll be judged mentally unsound and released."

Reese swallowed hard. She didn't want to hear the words. "And then?"

"And then Bertoller will find him, and they will begin rebuilding the hive."

"Can I stop them?"

"What do you think?"

She drew another deep breath. She had closed her eyes without realizing it—she opened them again. The being had changed. It was more indistinct now, still in the shape of a man but no longer bothering to ape David.

"Where am I?" she asked.

"Lost."

"How far will it take me to reach civilization? To get back to Jacob and Tyler?"

"You're assuming you will."

"Are you telling me I won't?"

The demon might have smiled—she couldn't see its features clearly enough to know. "People die in deserts. All the time."

"I can't die here. I have to get back to Jacob. I have to help him."

"You can . . . but not alone."

"I'm not alone," she answered, automatically, the words

turning to ash even as she spoke them. It was the watchword of the Oneness—not alone.

But who was with her now?

The Spirit, whom she could not touch?

Her cell, who had exiled her?

Tyler, Jacob, Richard, even Chris? Anyone? She was alone, alone in a desert where she could reach no one and might well, as the demon suggested, die.

The only help, the only companion presenting itself, was the demon in front of her.

And its counterparts that had been hounding her . . .

Or faithfully answering her call.

However you wanted to look at it.

She started to shake her head, almost violently, and called the sword back to her hand, stepping forward menacingly.

"Get away from me," she said.

"We are not on Bertoller's side," it said.

"Get away!"

It obliged, moving back suddenly and beginning to disperse into thin wisps of smoke. "We are power, and drawn to power. It doesn't matter what you ask of us. We make no judgments."

As it disappeared, escaping the slash of her sword, it said, "You need only call."

* * * * *

Tyler caught his breath as he slowed to a jog. Jacob hadn't waited for him and somehow managed to cross more ground in a few strides than Tyler could manage at a run. Why he was trying so hard to rejoin a man who had smashed him in the face, he wasn't really sure.

Jacob had finally slowed down, standing in the hollow between two sand dunes. He turned to face Tyler.

"If you come with me, you stay out of my way. And you do not interfere. Do you understand me?"

"Yes," Tyler said. "But what—"

"I am this close—this close—to avenging my wife, and a woman under my care, and countless—countless—others. Do you understand? I won't be stopped this time. I won't be delayed. I'm not going to be too late to cut Bertoller off from the source of his power because you separated me from my greatest weapon and dropped us in the middle of nowhere."

Tyler drew himself up short. "I dropped us? We fell. I didn't—"

"It was your arrogance that got us here," Jacob said. "You played with powers you don't understand and have no ability to control. Argue with that if you want."

He turned and began stalking away again. Tyler followed. "Wait. Did you call Reese a weapon?"

"Reese is a weapon. I don't expect you to see that."

"She's just a girl."

"She's a woman with an extraordinary gift and the capacity to become more powerful than you can dream. The demons have been offering themselves to her—giving themselves to her control. I have sought their power for twenty years, and they have never done that for me. She only needs to let go of her fears and her misguided beliefs about the Oneness. She does that, and she will become a force for good such as this world has rarely seen."

"By becoming a killer?" Tyler asked. "By killing Bertoller?"

"Bertoller must die."

"Bertoller is a man."

Jacob just cast a look over his shoulder that said Tyler was a worm, and stupider than a worm.

"What kind of game do you have around here?" he asked abruptly.

"What?"

"Game. Hunting animals."

"Deer," Tyler said. "And, uh, geese . . ."

"You still have that knife I gave you?"

"Yeah."

"Can you kill with it?"

"Not a deer or a goose. I'm a fisherman."

Jacob sighed. "Fine. Stay here. Gather wood for a fire. A big one."

"What are we going to do?"

"Call for help."

"With a fire? We're going to make smoke signals?"

Jacob glared at him scathingly. "I would like to believe you're not as ignorant as you pretend."

"I would like to believe you're not talking about calling the kind of help you're talking about calling."

"Just build the fire."

"Are you going to sacrifice something?"

"You're lucky I'm not going to sacrifice you."

Tyler looked around as though searching for help, but there wasn't much he could do. It couldn't really hurt to build a fire, could it? Jacob was already climbing the dune, off in search of something to kill—Good luck on that in the middle of the day, Tyler thought—and Tyler heaved a sigh and started to search for flammable scrub or driftwood.

He offered a prayer for Reese as he worked. He could still see her falling, hear her calling his name. What had happened back there?

And where was she?

"Be okay, Reese," he muttered as he began to fill his arms with driftwood. "Just be okay. We'll find you soon."

He paused.

"Please, remember that you aren't alone."

*   *   *   *   *

Bertoller watched as his men spread along the beach far below. Two others, armed thugs, bodyguards, stood at a respectful distance.

One of them carried a cell phone. It rang.

He waited as the thug grunted his way through the phone call and hung up.

"They've got the brat," he said. "And someone else. Young guy who won't give his name."

"Description?" Bertoller said.

"Early twenties, big. Red hair."

"Sawyer," Bertoller said. "That's good. If nothing else, he's a bargaining chip."

The phone rang again—this time the thug expressed surprise. When he hung up, he said, "They found the car Reese and Jacob were driving."

"Just the car?"

"It was empty, on the side of the road in the mountains. No sign of them—not a footprint, not nothing."

Bertoller considered that. It wasn't a good sign. And he was not happy to have lost them. Still, chances were they were heading for Lincoln—if word of Julie's death had reached them, it was guaranteed.

"They'll show up eventually."

The thug sounded nervous. "No word yet on the other woman."

Bertoller cursed in automatic response—not to the report, which was expected, but to the reminder. That Julie was alive somewhere, as the demons already gathered to him assured him was true, was his sharpest reminder that all was not yet under his control.

But the Power would win. No matter how many murder

victims came back to life and walked away.

He, the man whose name for some centuries had been Franz Bertoller, and before that names he could hardly remember, would not allow it to go any other way. He needed no reminder that the stakes were high—for him, deathly high. That for the first time in his history, he had been so thoroughly cut down that if he did not come back, if this tiny cell with its cluster of great powers that did not know themselves were able to strike at him again, he might lose entirely.

He might die.

He had spent his whole life serving the darkness, the chaos, the forces of entropy, corruption, and decay, but he would not surrender himself to those forces just yet.

He scanned the beach below for some sign of April, but it was too far, and wherever she was, she was hidden. Their ignorance of themselves had served him well thus far. April's mural was an alarm signal not only because it displayed what she was to him, but because it displayed it to herself as well. If she acted on what she saw herself to be, he would not be able to stand against her.

And she wasn't the only one. Richard. Reese. Melissa. Even the boy, Tyler.

He intended to kill them all before they could step out of their ignorance and into the fulness of their identities. Unless, of course, they turned—as David had, and Jacob, and nearly others. That had been his greatest dream. Turn the Oneness on itself, infiltrate and infect its ranks, turn it into a giant hive crawling with the powers of evil. Make the Oneness the ultimate destroyers of the universe they were holding together.

He had to admit now that he'd been overreaching.

But to kill a handful of great saints before they knew what they were? That, he could do. And doing so would empower him, make him stronger than he had been perhaps ever before.

He remembered great saints of the past, some he had killed and more he had kept his distance from, but he had never seen so many in one place.

From the beach below, a howl rose. Shouts carried the message up to him. The beast had found a trail.

Not the girl, not yet, but at least they could follow her now.

They were far from a village and farther from a real road. She wouldn't reach help or disappear anytime soon.

It could only be a matter of time before they found her.

Chris stared hard at their captors as they drove, watching them for some moment of weakness or inattention. Two sat in the front seat, two more were in the back with Chris, who sat with Miranda on his lap, which was all the room there was for her. He desperately hoped they'd be pulled over for a traffic violation.

Moments ago, one of the thugs had used a cell phone to call someone and report on their capture. It was clear from his wording that they'd expected to find Miranda and that they hadn't expected to find him.

"Come on," he said, ignoring the men next to him and talking to the ones up front—who he figured had seniority, or they would be the ones crammed into the backseat. "Where are you taking us? Who are you working for?"

"Can it," one of them said. "We don't answer to you."

"Who do you answer to?"

They ignored him. He knew he should consider himself lucky—they hadn't shot him dead on the farm ground, and they hadn't beat him up or otherwise made life miserable. But he had a very bad feeling about where things were going from here.

"Are you working for that creep Bertoller?"

Nothing, but he thought he saw a slight expression on one of their faces—just a twinge of satisfaction coupled with annoyance—that told him the answer was yes.

Richard had told him about the final conflict with Clint, the young man who had transformed before their eyes into a very old, very evil one—a man who hadn't been able to be pinned with Clint's crimes. It wasn't hard to figure he was behind the murder of Julie and now this kidnapping.

What was hard was knowing what to do next. If he'd been alone, he might have made a break for it already—just opened the car door and rolled. He was in as good a shape as any one of these goons and bet he was better at navigating the woods and countryside. But Miranda complicated things. He couldn't take her with him—the thought was ludicrous, given her penchant for hysterics—and he couldn't leave her behind.

Of course, chances were Reese would come and find them as she sought out Julie's "killers," so staying with these guys wouldn't mess up his plans to find her. But the thought of being collateral for the bad guys when she showed up was unacceptable.

And it was a bit galling to think of her rescuing him when he had been trying so hard to help her.

That was all assuming that Bertoller kept them alive long enough for Reese to find.

No guarantees, he figured.

So he really had to do something, and do it fast.

Inwardly he kicked himself for the giant blank his brain was drawing. Even as the car headed into a more populated area and other traffic began to fill the road, he couldn't think of any way out. He could try to signal to someone, but in such tight quarters, the goons would notice. Without any better ideas, he wedged one hand up against the window where his body and Miranda's blocked it from view and tried to wave down another car, but the only motions he could make without drawing attention were so small that he doubted any other driver on the road would notice it either.

When Miranda first announced that she needed the bathroom, he wanted to kiss her.

She was brilliant. Or, he realized, just really, really naive. And self-focused.

It wasn't a ploy—she really had to go. And she kept up a litany of complaints, to the silence of their captors, until finally the driver burst out, "Fine! We'll stop! But no monkey business, you understand me? You'll go and come right back, and if you take a step to run away, we will run you down. You understand me?"

"Yes," she said, trembling, and he pulled over. Chris and Miranda both spilled out the side of the car at once, so tightly wedged in that it was almost impossible to get one out without the other.

To Chris's overwhelming joy, the opposite door swung open and the two goons from the backseat started to climb out on the other side—apparently wanting to breathe the air and stretch as badly as he did. As they were climbing out, Miranda ventured forward to a handy bush, the driver said something to direct her, and for a moment, all eyes were on her.

Chris ran.

He hadn't even exactly been planning it; it just happened. His legs churned and his heart raced, and he was off, running straight for the woods only fifty yards away. Shouts and bullets followed him, the shots pinging off the dirt on either side but missing. He heard a long, loud wail—Miranda, not happy to be abandoned.

"I'll be back, kid," he said through gritted teeth as he vaulted a ditch and landed in the cover of the trees. The jump knocked him off balance for a moment, and he scrambled back to his feet and just kept running. Branches pulled at his shirt and whipped his face; he kept going. Eyes forward. Legs running. His whole body straining deeper into the wooded darkness, farther from his pursuers.

He heard feet pounding the ground behind him and grunts as the men vaulted the ditch. Branches snapped and cracked, but the goons were wearing suits, and the branches were snagging in their jackets and slowing them down worse than they were doing for Chris—or so he assumed from the cursing and the distance of their voices. He didn't look back.

His ears told him only two of the men had chased him; the other two must still be at the car with Miranda. He kept on straight ahead until he could tell they were almost on him, and then, picking a tiny clearing, he stopped on a dime, turned, and grabbed one man by the scruff of his neck, using his own momentum to throw him off his feet and straight forward. The man's head collided with a tree trunk, and he was down. Chris had already met the other one with an uppercut to the jaw. The thug brought his gun up, but they were at close quarters, and Chris managed to grab his arm, twist, and force him to drop the gun. Chris ducked, grabbed the gun, and shot the man in the leg. The other seemed to be out cold.

"You should tell your boss to call goon school and get them to send out a couple of new students," Chris said. "You two are an embarrassment." He mopped sweat from his forehead with his T-shirt, noting that blood came away from it. Danged tree branches. For good measure, he shot the unconscious man behind the knee.

The second man was holding his leg and seething with rage, his eyes almost black with it.

"You better hope you get a week off for that," Chris said, nodding at him. "Otherwise I'll likely be seeing you soon. Doubt you'll like it."

Gun in hand, he turned and stalked back into the woods.

* * * * *

When she couldn't swim anymore, April returned to the beach and ran. She could sense the beast gaining on her. She could feel its spiritual presence—a dark, pulsating blot—although waves crashing and her own heart pounding in her ears blocked out the sounds of pursuit.

She wasn't going to escape this way. She knew that.

So she stopped running. Just quit, and let herself drop onto the sandy beach and sit among the sharp-edged grass and wait.

A comparison from her childhood suggested itself to her: hiding in the closet, waiting for the rage she could hear throughout the house to find her, knowing it most likely would. Knowing the futility of trying to run.

But this didn't feel like that, somehow.

The voice she had heard in the dark place beneath the waves had gripped her heart too firmly, and she felt safe in that grip. As though this time, she was not the child, but the adult waiting for a child to rage out its own temper until it dropped in exhaustion.

Somehow, it felt right to stop and wait for it. Like this was not only the only thing she could do, but the best thing.

She had rounded a cliff bend and could hear the monster gaining, about to burst upon her. Her sword formed in her hand, and she regarded it wryly—only weeks ago, she had led a quiet life as part of a village cell where nothing ever happened. Practicing the art of painting had not given her much ability in warfare. And for all that her painting seemed to be a gift of staggering meaning and magnitude, she couldn't see any way to turn it against the beast about to burst around the corner.

It did so a moment later and paused as if confused as to her whereabouts—for one moment she thought it might rush past without seeing her.

No such luck.

Yellow eyes focused in on her and narrowed. This was not— exactly—a demon. Demonically driven, yes, but the creature was something else, lacking a demon's purpose or intelligence. Her blood ran cold when she realized it might just tear her apart before any of her other pursuers arrived.

"Spirit, save me," she said, moving into a crouch with her sword held defensively before her. She had no idea what she was doing, but she knew there were fighter instincts in there somewhere—hopefully they would kick in with enough force to make some difference.

The beast let out a roar and charged forward. April sprang up and dodged the charge, managing to whirl around and deal the animal a whack with her blade before it realized it had missed her. The blow bounced off its thick hide, and she wondered if she'd just made it mad.

"Come on," she said, crouching low to make herself a tense, ready-to-spring target. The ocean waves washed up on the shore behind her, lapping at her feet. "Get this over with."

To her surprise, the beast stalked from side to side but didn't attack. It eyed her sword warily—perhaps aware that it was capable of doing more damage than she'd demonstrated.

Or maybe, she thought, it was afraid of the water.

Inspired by that thought, she backed further into the waves, wading out to her knees. She was at a disadvantage here—if she tried to move quickly she'd probably just be knocked over by the pull of the water—but the beast wasn't coming any closer.

"If you only knew," she said, "how little threat I actually am."

"Thankfully," another voice said, "we do know that."

She straightened out of her crouch and lowered her sword as the men came around the bend, six of them, armed. Two of them went after the beast with a leash made of chain links; the others stalked into the water toward April.

"Don't try to run," the leader announced.

"If you didn't notice, I'm not," she said.

This time the men produced more chains, with fetters, and April sighed as her sword dissolved. She held her hands out and let them bind her. The leader approached and nodded at the chains.

"That's for the trouble you caused us," he said. He motioned toward the beast. "You're smart, I'll give you that . . . don't know how you knocked him off his course, but it's a good thing for all of us you did."

"What exactly do you get out of this?" April asked. "I doubt you're doing this for giggles."

The man smiled. He was younger than some of the others, maybe thirty-five, but his face was scarred and his eyes were hard. "What do you think I get? Lots and lots of money."

"Is that worth it? I'm not the only one you're going to hurt if you work with Bertoller."

"Do you think I mind hurting people?"

She gave up trying to talk to him as he grabbed her arm and shoved her forward, barely catching her when she stumbled in the waves. To them, her escape had to look like sheer annoyance—a mad dash for freedom that had availed her nothing and cost them time and energy in chasing her.

They had no idea how much the escape actually had availed her—how much the encounter underwater had changed things for her.

Even she didn't really have much of an idea of that.

She only knew that it had. And in the confidence of that knowledge, she found that she was not afraid.

* * * * *

Chris's fingers shook with adrenaline as he dialled a number on the pay phone, praying this would work. It was his third call—the first to Lieutenant Jackson, who promised to send out cops to look for Miranda, the second to information to get this number.

Someone picked up. A man.

"Is this Andrew Hunter?" Chris asked.

"Yes. Who is this?"

"My name is Chris Sawyer. I don't have a lot of time to explain, but sir, someone has your daughter."

"My . . . who is this?"

"I want to help her, but I need a car and someone to back me up. Can you meet me?" He named the little town where he'd found himself when he emerged from the woods, a forty-five-minute drive from Lincoln.

"I'll be there," Hunter said.

Chris specified a meeting place—across the street, at the post office where he'd spotted several fairly big men working. Might as well add extra backup if Bertoller's men tracked him somehow.

He hoped reaching out to Andrew Hunter was the right thing to do. He knew nothing about the man.

He just knew that if he was a father, and his daughter was in trouble, he would want to know. Would have a right to know. A right that Jacob had been denying this man far too long.

Andrew Hunter arrived half an hour later—having sped all the way from Lincoln, if Chris had to guess. He was tall, fit, even athletic, but with an earnest expression and glasses that gave him a bookish air. He cut straight to the chase.

"What do you know about my daughter? What's going on?"

"Miranda's been kidnapped," Chris said. "I want to find her, but I'll need your help."

It was a long story, and Chris told it, keeping his voice low, while they drank coffee in a small cafe next to the post office. Hunter clutched his cup like a lifeline when Chris referenced Julie's being shot—"although the eyewitness says she wasn't killed," he said, fudging the story a bit. It might be better not to bring up strange lights and resurrections at this stage of the game.

"When I saw the news about Julie, I didn't know what to think. I've been trying to reach her for years," Hunter said when Chris stopped. "Called, sent letters. I even tried to see her—three times—but she wouldn't come out of the house. The third time they just ran me off the property."

"It's possible she didn't know you were there," Chris said, choosing his words carefully. "The man leading that group—"

"Jacob," Andrew said bitterly. "The man who ruined my life."

"Him. I'm not sure he told Julie you were writing. I found your letters in a file cabinet in his office. That's how I knew to contact you."

Andrew stared into his coffee cup, and Chris continued. "Miranda certainly didn't know—she thinks you're dead. She was with me when I found the files, but I didn't tell her . . . figured it was better for her to find out under different circumstances."

"I'll do whatever it takes to get her back," Andrew said.

Chris smiled. "Yeah. I thought you would."

"But why call me? Why not call the police?"

"I did call the police," Chris said, "but I'm going in on my own too. I've tangled with these people before, and the police aren't . . . well. There are unusual circumstances. I wanted someone to back me whose stakes were as high as mine."

"You found the right man," Andrew said, fervently. "Stakes . . . what are yours?"

"The girl I love," Chris said.

Andrew reached across the table, and they shook—a firm, strong handshake.

"I'll do whatever you need. Tell me what's first."

"First . . ." Chris hesitated. "First, I give you the lowdown on the extenuating circumstances. These guys we're going after are not just thugs. They're plugged into some kind of spiritual power, and they're going after more of it."

Andrew nodded. "Sounds like Jacob."

"What do you know about Jacob?" Chris asked.

Andrew's face flushed. "That he's dangerous and the worst kind of thief. And very convincing and charming. He almost talked both of us into joining his community—Julie and me. We liked the rural aspect, and the way of life he was teaching—it was simple, cleaner somehow than what we were used to. But then he started sharing with me more of what he was into, just 'man to man,' he said. He was trying to harness some kind of spiritual power, and it was dark. I said I wanted nothing to do with it. Next I knew, Julie said she was leaving me and joining the community, and she accused me of betraying Jacob and falsely accusing him. He got to her somehow. Don't know how, but he did." He clenched his fists on the table. "When I heard about Julie being killed . . ."

"Jacob didn't shoot her," Chris said. "But I won't tell you he's innocent. She got into trouble because of him. But listen, I've got good reason to believe Julie is alive. After we get Miranda back, I'll help you find her too."

"Thank you," Andrew said. "Anything I can do for you . . . you just tell me."

"I've got a few people I want to find," Chris said. "I just might take you up on that."

"So," Andrew said, "where do we start? Do you know where those men have taken Miranda?"

"No."

"Do you know how to contact them?"

"No, not that either. And I don't think they're interested in talking to me, so we shouldn't expect ransom notes."

Andrew looked frustrated. "So how were you planning to get started?"

"By asking someone who will know where she is." Chris paused. "Someone with watchers everywhere."

Tyler stared wide-eyed as Jacob dragged the animal into the cleft between the dunes where he had stacked firewood. It wasn't a deer—not big enough. Some kind of goat, he realized. It was still alive, and kicking feebly.

"This is wrong," he said, a salt breeze blowing in his face. Jacob ignored him, still dragging the goat toward the pile of wood. "This is wrong!" he said, louder this time.

Jacob answered. "I am doing what I have to do. Don't get in the way."

He hauled the goat up and landed it heavily atop the stack of wood.

"You really think this is going to work?" Tyler squeaked.

Jacob glared at him, fiery-eyed. "Clam up and help me light the fire. No words—I don't want you saying something that will mess it up."

Tyler hesitantly moved to Jacob's side, and the bigger man

clamped a hand on his arm. He stared up into his eyes.

"No prayer. You understand me? You start reaching for the Spirit, and you will lose my chance to reach the help I need."

Tyler wanted to say, He would answer you too.

If you'd let him.

But he didn't say it. He wasn't sure it was true.

Tyler felt his breath coming faster as Jacob searched his pockets for matches. The air was starting to darken, as it had when the flock had gathered overhead in the mountains. He could feel presences, personalities, wills, in the darkness, and they made his skin crawl.

It didn't matter what Jacob said—he couldn't let this happen.

"You can't do this," he said, raising his voice to make sure Jacob heard him.

"Shut. Up."

"You can't. You're Oneness. You start playing with demons, and you're going to make something terrible happen. This is wrong, Jacob. You have to stop it."

Tyler balled his hands into fists and stepped forward, ready to throw himself at the older, bigger man, and probably get the beating of his life. All he knew was that Jacob couldn't be allowed to do this, and if Tyler was here for any reason, it was to stop him.

Jacob found matches and bent to get the fire started, ignoring Tyler.

So he did the one thing Jacob had commanded him not to do.

Prayed.

"Spirit!" he said loudly. Almost shouted. "Spirit, come and stop this! Come and carry us out of here!"

He could feel opposition in the air around him—the invisible spirits squirming and glaring and protesting his action.

"We are your sons!" Tyler called. "Come and help us!"

Jacob launched himself at him.

The expression in his eyes was murderous.

Tyler jumped out of his way and circled to the other side of the pyre, still calling. "Come and stop this! Please, help us!"

The darkness around them grew thick as pitch and threatened to suffocate Tyler where he stood. The goat began to bleat frantically.

Without thinking, just somehow inspired, he closed the gap between himself and Jacob, grabbed Jacob's shirt, and hauled him upward, shouting, "This is my brother! Don't leave him behind!"

He didn't even know when he had realized his feet were leaving the ground, that he was being pulled up, out, free of the black air and the creatures filling it. But it was happening—and with his hands full of Jacob's cotton shirt, he was hauling the bigger man along with them.

* * * * *

The shadows over the desert were deepening.

Reese wasn't even sure how that was possible—she couldn't see clouds in the sky, and surely not enough hours had passed for it to be evening. Yet, her surroundings were growing darker.

More ominous.

Once again, she wondered what had happened—how she had ended up here. She thought the demons must have dragged her down.

The landscape was anything but smooth, and she found herself picking through boulder fields, dodging thorny scrub, and struggling up and down inclines as much as travelling smoothly. She could still see the mountains off in the distance, orienting her to the points of the compass, and kept struggling southwest, trying to move toward the coast and toward Lincoln at the same time.

She had to get there—had to find Bertoller, stop him, avenge Julie, help Jacob.

If Jacob made it there himself. Who knew? Maybe what had happened to her had happened to Tyler and Jacob too. Maybe the Spirit had simply dropped them, and they had fallen— maybe no one had been there to catch them.

The darkness of her own thoughts frightened her.

She worked her way up a slope that dropped sharply off on the other side, leading into an empty creek bed.

She stumbled at the sight that met her eyes.

Chris was there, sitting with his back against the bank, waiting for her.

"What's taken you so long?" he asked. "I've been waiting for you."

Why was he smiling? And why was she so thirsty?

"Chris?"

"Who do you think I am? Santa Claus?"

"No," she said, slowly, her tongue thick in her mouth. "No, I think you're one of them. Again."

Her sword had formed in her hand.

As automatic a response to demonic presence as swallowing to a mouthful of water.

Chris's form didn't change, but something in his eyes did—they hollowed and went dark. She was glad—she wasn't sure she could handle Chris's eyes right now.

"We can bring you together," the demon said in Chris's voice.

"I don't need your help."

"We would not keep you apart. We don't need your loyalty. We only want to serve."

She closed her eyes. "Shut up."

"He really is searching for you."

Her eyes snapped open. "Where? Where is he?"

"Oh, now you want our help."

She didn't think this was the same demon she had talked to earlier, in David's body—this one was more mocking.

On the good side, that took away from the sting of its words—a little. It felt like talking to an enemy.

But maybe that was part of the point—putting an enemy

in Chris's body. Just to underscore the conflict she'd always felt about him. She wanted to love Chris. Wanted to be loved by him. Was loved by him—at least, she thought she was.

But she was Oneness, and he was not, and that made their love impossible in any romantic sense.

A fact she hated.

Romance wasn't usual to the Oneness anyway. The connection between all was so deep that it made marriage almost superfluous. But it happened now and again. And was life-changing when it did.

It was partly why Jacob's loss of his first wife had been so deep, so horrendous. And why she wanted to help him bring Bertoller to justice.

She could not imagine losing Chris, and they were not even anything more than friends.

"I'm afraid his search for you isn't going well," the demon said, the hollow eyes eerie in Chris's face.

"What are you talking about?"

"Someone may have found him first."

"Someone?" Her blood ran cold. "Bertoller?"

"Oh, now you want our help?" The demon was fading, Chris's form disappearing from before her eyes. She wanted to reach out, hold him there, stop the disintegration.

She almost begged it not to go.

It was gone. She dropped to her knee in the creek bed, laying her crutch down beside her, and allowed herself to wish for water, for Chris, for help.

Where was Chris? And what was happening to him?

And why—why—was she so alone?

The air was still darkening. Almost as though smoke were filling it, but there was no smell, no taste, no clouds. Only shadows and deepening dark.

Her whole body hurt. Her leg ached from the ankle up, and she was sore and bruised from fighting and walking and stumbling and just from loneliness and anger and frustration, hang it.

But it didn't even matter. It didn't matter how she felt. She just had to find Jacob—and now Chris. She just had to make something, anything right.

She just had to bring Bertoller down.

And David.

The last thought took a moment to even register.

Why had she thought that?

Why did she care what happened to David?

Because the demon had said he was just going to be released. They wouldn't even keep him in prison. And he would go right back to destroying others, like he had destroyed her, and he wouldn't even pay . . .

He wouldn't even pay.

She stared her own heart in the mirror as those words repeated themselves.

"So that's what this is all about?" she said aloud. "You want revenge."

Silence. Nothing in her argued back. She just let the words sink in, let them hang in the air.

"That's why you keep calling demons," she told herself. "Because you want revenge. Because you haven't forgiven him. You're a walking demon magnet."

She laughed—surprised at the bitterness in her own tone. She was dragging the demons around behind her on a chain of bitterness, refusing to let it go.

And that meant, somehow, she had let the darkness into her own heart. That chaos was eating away at her, cankering her soul, ulcerating what was left of the Spirit in her life.

Yes. She had felt that. The hollow at the core of who she was—the growing distance from the Oneness—the pain that would not go away.

"But I need to be healed!" she cried out. "I can't just . . . can't just let it go."

She found herself doubled over, arms wrapped around her stomach where the hollow was, the massive, gaping hole that wanted to swallow her from the inside. Around her, it was dark as night. A cry started from somewhere deep within her and rose, climbing in volume until it shook her as she loosed it, a long cry of pain and rage.

There were faces gathering in the darkness, looming over her. One figure, tall and broad, stood before her with bear-like, clawed hands spread out on either side of her head. Offering her vision once again.

"Show me," she choked out.

The hands closed on either side of her.

She saw April first—running along a beach, with a massive, muscled beast bounding behind her. As she watched, the beast leaped and brought April down, its claws skewering her shoulders. Men followed, carrying chains and guns.

Then she saw Julie shot in an alley at night, city lights illuminating the scene, falling, dead.

She saw Miranda crying, wailing, squirming in a desperate attempt to get away from men who held both her arms—

And then Chris, being chased through the woods. As she watched, bullets whizzed through the air behind him and burst through his chest, too many to count, and he sprawled dead on the ground.

"No!" she heard herself shouting. "No!"

Then Tyler, with his hands bound, and something happening—a bonfire, a sacrifice.

She saw the cell house in the fishing village burning, swallowed in billows of black smoke.

She saw Bertoller shoot Jacob at point-blank range.

And David was there, watching in the background. Free. And approving like he had been when Patrick died.

"Get me out of here!" she shouted. "I need to help them!"

Julie's death was already in the past, too late to help. But surely not all of these visions had already come to pass. Surely there was time to help. There was something she could do.

"Get me somewhere I can help," she said.

One of the faces in the shadows around her said, "Anything else we can do?"

"Yes," she said, violently wiping tears from her face. "Heal this stupid leg. Get me out of this cast."

"You're asking for our help?"

"Yes. I need it. Help me."

Her ears filled with a roar as the spirits inhabiting the air moved to do as she asked.

* * * * *

Melissa was playing the piano like the song would save someone. She had been three hours at it, filling the house with music.

They'd heard nothing from April and had no lead on where to look for her. They had gathered to pray, the only thing they could do, and Melissa poured her prayers out in music.

The Spirit was a great calm, a deep dark. Richard had hoped to tap into knowledge, or power; into the rush he often felt when he went deep in prayer. But there was only this—

Only stillness.

The circumstances were too familiar for them not to make the connection: last time April had disappeared, she had been abducted by thugs and left in a cave to die, starved to death because of who she was—a great saint. An identity she had not yet truly embraced and walked in. That event had led to their meeting Reese, and the battle with the hive in Lincoln.

They had thought the battle was over.

And now here it was, beginning again—in the same place.

But this time, the Spirit was still.

Richard felt almost estranged from it. As though the plan the Spirit was willing into being this time was something he could not accept.

Melissa played on.

Was death the Spirit's will?

Melissa's death, April's. Was that the meaning of this stillness? Because this time, the Spirit would do nothing to stop what was pending?

For the first time, Richard found himself so disturbed by what he was sensing that he had to stop praying. He stood, nodded to Mary, and left the house. The strains of Melissa's song followed him out.

His feet took him down the road in the fading light of evening, over the cobblestones toward the bay. The moon was already out, thin and shining in a blue sky; a planet, nearby, shone more brightly than the brightest stars.

"I can't do this," he said aloud. "Can't just give up and let them die." He groaned. "You're asking too much."

Trust me, he thought he heard, spoken by a voice deep in his spirit.

But the words brought no comfort, no peace.

He did not know how to trust—not when there was nothing he could do. Not when he was being asked to lay down everything, even to put down prayer, to accept that it would avail him nothing.

He had spent years learning to operate in the Spirit. To drink it in, to fall into the river, to be carried by it, to act in its surging power.

He felt now as if it had cast him ashore.

"You're asking too much," he said again.

He found himself on the docks, looking over the water of the bay. A vast expanse of blue covering who knew what mysteries beneath its waves. Giving not even a hint of what lay beyond the waters.

April's painting came to his mind's eye: the illumination above the bay. But the only light he could see now was the sickle moon.

And it, too, offered no answers.

Someone was there beside him.

He thought it was Mary. She was always faithful to seek him out in times like these—times when he most needed someone to stand by his side.

He turned to acknowledge her presence, but it wasn't her.

It was no one.

And yet there was someone there.

He felt himself beginning to tremble.

Back up at the house, Melissa let her hands grow still, and the music ceased.

Tyler didn't know how long the journey took. Nor did he know exactly how it happened. There were no flaming horses this time, just a passage of time that occurred beyond any conscious sense, and then they were dumped in the street in a city he recognized as Lincoln. And Reese was there, staring at them with a disturbance in her eyes—a darkness, a tornado—that scared him.

He half-expected Jacob to go after him then and there, but lying on his back in the street, Jacob took in the skyline and realized where they were. He kept quiet. Maybe for Reese's sake; Tyler didn't really know. He was convinced that he'd made an enemy. Which was ironic, because for the first time, he truly understood how much he and Jacob were One. That what he had shouted to the Spirit was true. This man was his brother, and he wanted to save him.

He also realized, for the first time, how much danger Jacob was actually in.

"I know this neighbourhood," Reese said, turning. "The safe house is near here. Where Julie was."

She was walking—her cast was gone. Tyler decided not to ask her about it. He suspected he wouldn't like the answer.

"Then this is where we'll pick up Bertoller's trail," Jacob said, rising from the ground and markedly ignoring Tyler. "We need to talk to the people at the . . ."

"You can't," Reese said. "They're looking for you, remember?"

"They'll be looking for you, too," Tyler said. "You're the one who took Jacob out."

He was right, and they all knew it.

Before Tyler could wrap his mind fully around what was happening, he'd been elected to seek out the trail. He found himself walking two streets over from the safe house, listening to the buzz of activity still happening over there and trying to figure out what he was going to say that would convince anyone to talk to him.

In the circumstances, he felt alone, and he hated that.

Concentrating on steadying his breath, he focused on the police cars and the flashing lights up ahead. Did these people always do everything like a big show? They'd been here since the night before, hadn't they? So there shouldn't be any reason for lights and attention-getting. But there they were. Maybe it was necessary to look intimidating so they could keep interference from the population away.

He didn't think they were going to welcome him.

He was half a block away when the hilt started to form in his hand, and instinctively he knew he wasn't going to have to deal with the police after all.

Someone else was here, and someone else wanted to talk to him.

He heard a low hiss from a house right beside him, coming from the cellar, like a gas leak. The cellar door, an old-fashioned outdoor wooden affair, was open, beckoning him into a black pit.

Surely they didn't think he was that stupid.

And yet he wanted to talk to them. He was sure they were here waiting for him to give him a message, and he needed to hear that message or else he and Jacob and Reese would keep chasing their tails until they gave up in exhaustion and Bertoller killed who knew how many other innocent people, starting with everyone from the farm community and moving on.

Not that he expected them to tell him the truth. He just wanted to hear the lie so they could get to work seeing through it. The Spirit had brought him straight here, so he meant to follow up in whatever way he could.

A tree branch, stretched out overhead just low enough to avoid power lines and thus being cut by city officials, but dry and dead enough that it should have been cut, creaked and moaned as it moved in the wind.

Except there was no wind.

The sword finished forming in his hand. He hoped none of the people up at the crime scene would look his way and see him standing there, looking like a comic book wannabe staring down an invisible enemy.

"Come out," he said, spreading his feet a little apart so they wouldn't start taking him to the cellar of their own volition. "I'm not talking to you down there."

His voice shook a little, but he held his ground. And felt proud of himself.

You weren't going to catch him going down into that darkness. The demons could come out and face him like a man.

Something almost filmy started to appear in the air before him. He recalled as quickly as he could what little he actually knew about these creatures. Ordinarily they possessed in order to take physical form and have power in the physical world. For them to take on substance of their own, they needed to feed off of something—some evil, some great wrongdoing.

Something like the murder of a woman like Julie.

He could hardly see this one, but it was there, hovering with a bare substance that was almost too ethereal to see. If he blinked, it took him a moment to get hold of its shape again. He felt as though he was trying to fix his eyes on a rising wisp of smoke that was blowing away even as he spoke with it.

But he heard its voice clearly, speaking into the air. This was no voice in his head. It was outside him, disembodied but belonging to a real personality.

But the voice said nothing. It just laughed at him.

"Why are you here?" Tyler demanded, afraid to raise his voice too loud—he still didn't want to attract attention from the crew up the street. Didn't want anyone normal to see him down here, confronting a demon in broad daylight with a sword in his hand. He tried to keep his voice strong and authoritative even if it was kind of quiet.

The demon laughed again.

"What do you have to tell me? Why are you here?"

"What makes you think I want to talk to you?" the voice answered.

Tyler reddened. "I'm all you've got. I'll take a message. Just give it to me."

"Come to the haunting ground," it said.

And even Tyler knew what those words meant.

* * * * *

"The haunting ground," Reese said.

"That's what it said."

She exchanged glances with Jacob, who seemed both excited and angry.

"The cemetery," she said aloud.

"Of course," Jacob said. His tone was dismissive. She didn't need to speak the words—they'd all understood the reference.

Bertoller would meet them in the cemetery Jacob had haunted for years as a young man—the cemetery where Bertoller's own gravestone stood, lying for decades about his death.

That seemed appropriate.

"They're going to be waiting for us," Reese said. "Ready for us. We're talking about walking into a trap."

"Waiting for us, yes," Jacob said. "Ready for us, no. Not this time."

"Why do you say that?" Tyler asked at the same time Reese did.

Tyler got the distinct impression Jacob was only answering Reese. "Because we will do things they don't believe we will. Because I will use whatever powers I must use. Because you will kill Bertoller. And they believe we are still bound by the Oneness."

Reese met his eyes without flinching, even as Tyler waited for her to rebuff Jacob's words, to tell him how wrong he was. About everything. But she didn't say a word.

"Reese . . ." Tyler said.

"I'll do what I have to do," Reese said. She turned and let her eyes meet Tyler's. There was something new in them—she was apologetic, but determined.

He shook his head. "No, Reese. If you play his game—you don't know what you're getting into."

"I'm afraid I do," she said. "I'm afraid I'm already into this too deep to turn back."

He asked the question through building dread. "How did you get here?"

"I used . . . whatever powers I had to use."

Something in his heart broke. "Reese, don't give in to them. Whatever they're telling you, it's lies."

"There's too much at stake," Reese said. "I'm sorry, Tyler. But right now, Bertoller is positioned to take everything I care about, and I can't lose all that. Not again."

"You're giving it to him," Tyler said, tears filling his eyes. "To them."

"You don't understand," she said, and turned away.

To keep him from seeing tears in her own eyes, he thought.

"You believed like me once," he said.

Her back went rigid against the backdrop of the neighbour-hood lights. "I'm not that person anymore, Tyler. And that was a long time ago. Just pray for me. I can't. So do it for me."

"I will."

Jacob took Reese's arm. "Let's go," he said. "There's no sense in wasting time."

Tyler took a step after them, but Jacob turned and pinned him with his eyes. "You're not coming."

"Excuse me?"

"You're not coming. I can't trust you."

"I got us here!"

"You went against my orders and interfered with my plans. I needed that power for more reasons than just getting us here. And you'll interfere with Reese if you get half a chance. You've proven yourself. I'm not taking you another step."

"Reese!"

She just shook her head. "He's right, Tyler. Better you stay here anyway. You'll be safer."

She allowed herself to meet his gaze, and he saw clearly the tears in her eyes. "Just pray, Tyler. Get us any help you can any way you can. But don't come. I don't want you in that cemetery tonight."

* * * * *

Franz Bertoller stood on a gravestone and watched the preparations unfolding in the moonlight and the flickering shadows cast by the torches ringing one small area of the grounds. They would do things right, this time.

His own gravestone, engraved with his name and a death date twenty years earlier, shone in the moonlight. A massive slab of granite, he had designed it as an altar, though few knew it. It had been used once before: the night of his "death" when he renewed his youth and continued on with a new face and a new name.

But the sacrifice that night would pale in power compared to the one he would offer tonight.

His men, dressed in black and barely distinguishable from the shadows, went about their work silently, bringing bundles of sticks and kindling and laying them on the growing pile on the altar. Chickens and goats clucked and bleated from the crates that had already been delivered, outside of the torchlit area in the center of the cemetery.

A car pulled up outside of the cemetery, announced by the purr of its engine and the flash of headlights. Bertoller nearly stood on tiptoe, suddenly alert in every cell, to see if this was the delivery he was waiting for.

It wasn't. Four men approached with a girl Bertoller recognized as Julie's daughter.

"Put her back there," he said, nodding toward the animal crates. "You'll be able to find a crate for her."

The girl was blubbering and crying, and Bertoller turned away in disgust. She would be the height of the preliminary sacrifices, and her youth and innocence would make her worth more than some, but nothing in comparison to the climax of the night.

Another car arrived.

He smiled.

This was the one.

He'd heard reports from the first time they abducted this one: she had panicked and tried to fight back, and they had knocked her out and dumped her in the cave. She was terrified, they said. Easy prey.

Nothing like a great saint.

Moreover, the girl they had cornered in the cave, the one who had thrown herself off the cliff and led them on a chase along the coast, had been driven by fear.

So he was a little shaken to see her now, as they brought her into the torchlight with her hands in chains.

Something had changed.

She met his eyes without hesitation, her expression challenging him, asking why he had brought her here, insisting that he examine himself and think twice about his actions.

He pulled his hands into nail-gouging fists.

She had come into her own. This was a great saint.

And at last, she knew it.

"You're too late," he said, answering the words she didn't say. "You've realized it too late. Just in time to give your power to me—to feed the darkness."

"What you're about to do—demons themselves would be afraid to do it."

"But I am not a coward."

"Only a fool."

Her eyes did not flinch away from his. "You aren't the only one who will die tonight," he said. "We will make a beautiful fire, and the Power himself will light it."

"Whatever you're planning to do, you're going to regret it," April said. "You can't win this fight—after all this time, you should know that. All of your efforts are going to come to nothing, to backfire. Starting here."

"You presume to lecture me?"

"I presume to tell you the truth. It's not too late for you."

He laughed at that. "You are deluded."

"There will be a fire here tonight," April said. "But it may not be the one you intend to light. Please, listen to me . . . it isn't too late. You can turn around."

Too late, he realized how much power she was exercising over the whole scene—that everyone was listening to her, every one of his thugs, that Miranda had ceased her wailing, that even the animals had quieted. That he himself was allowing this woman to speak and to extend grace to him.

As though she had the authority to do so.

As though she could speak, and forgiveness would be his, and a new life.

And he didn't know how to stop her. Every violent impulse that normally ran through his body, every sadistic command he would usually delight to give, felt now like the height of lunacy.

He had felt this before, only when tangling with the great

saints.

He did understand why the demons feared to kill them directly.

Nevertheless, her death would accomplish everything he needed, and it would do it quickly. He had no choice.

The sense of threat only heightened the reality of that.

"It's not too late for any of you," April announced, "but you will cross a line eventually. Don't go there tonight. Save yourselves while you still can!"

"Be quiet," Bertoller said. He was shaking, and he hopped off the stone and advanced on her, holding his finger in front of her face. "Be silent."

He didn't say the word throbbing behind his demands:

Please.

Please be quiet, now, before you do too much damage.

To his surprise, she obeyed. Except for three last words:

"Not even you."

He jerked his head to the side, where a tree stood. His men took her and began to chain her to it. She would die, finally, on the flames on the altar. But first she would watch the others killed.

She was horribly unafraid.

He remembered a woman, hundreds of years ago, whom he had starved to death in his less courageous—or desperate—days. She had been like this. The word "courage" was not even enough. She simply lacked any fear. As though she knew something he didn't.

He had never forgotten her. Teresa, her name was. He had been a younger man then.

Part of him had fallen in love with her.

But choices had to be made, and it was power, not love, that won the day. When the Power, the being at the source of all that fuelled him, demanded her life, he gave it.

That was the day he lost his soul.

He had learned that day that in a human sacrifice, far more was lost than the life of one human being. Forces were loosed that could not be controlled. As his men continued to build up the pyre, he thought briefly of the consequences of centuries of playing with fire.

He wanted to get started.

"Where is he?" he snapped, talking to his second-in-command—the tall, scarred young man who had brought April in. He didn't know the man's name. He didn't care.

"They're bringing him."

"Call them. Tell them to speed it up."

"Surely you don't want to start now? Shouldn't you wait till midnight?"

"We'll do it properly," he snapped. "Don't lecture me on my own business."

Yes, the final sacrifice would have to wait for midnight—it was the hour of greatest power. But there was no reason they could not begin the rituals now. Begin the processes that would steal his attention again, return his mind and his heart to the task at hand.

Just as soon as the last remaining sacrifice arrived.

* * * * *

Chris didn't know why he felt it was necessary to leave the town, but he did. So dragging a questioning and confused Andrew behind him, he drove outside of the town, found a barren stretch of ground on top of a ridge with city lights twinkling below, and pulled over.

He got out of the car and stood at the edge of the ridge. Overhead, a thin moon lit the sky with a surprisingly bright light. A planet sparkled beside it, and other stars were beginning to come out, clear and lucid in an atmosphere that felt especially translucent tonight.

He heard a car door shut as Andrew climbed out of the truck, but he stayed back.

Chris cleared his throat.

"All right," he said. "This is not exactly a surrender. But I will admit one thing, because I have to: I can't do this without your help."

Nothing happened. No answer, no movement, no apparition appearing before him.

"I know you're out there," Chris continued, "and I know that somehow, you're influencing things. I know you have eyes everywhere, because at least one of them has been watching me—and is watching me right now, I'm pretty sure, which means you can also hear me. I know you care as much as I do about what's happening. I know you care that Miranda is in that hideous joke of a man's hands. And that Reese is in some kind of trouble, and that she's probably heading to corner the same man. And you know perfectly well that I can't find them. That I've been searching all this time and now I've lost the trail and I don't know where to find anyone or how to help them, and I don't think I have much time left."

Still nothing.

Except . . . now he had the unnerving sensation, as undeniable as it was intangible, that someone was listening.

"So, since we are on the same side at least for the moment, I am asking for your help. Please show me where Miranda is, and where Reese is. And help me rescue them."

The stars continued to shine—brighter, if that was possible. The city lights winked below. The air was dry, cool, and still.

It was, maybe, rude to talk to someone without addressing them.

So he said it.

"Spirit. I need your help."

He felt it on his skin for a bare instant—heat. Then sudden, searing heat—and in the next moment, a warmth had settled around his heart, constricting, strengthening, and momentarily making him unable to breathe.

In the next moment the child was there. The eerie, silent child who had been watching him. He was standing on the ridge next to Chris.

"You aren't the Spirit," Chris said, which was stupid but he couldn't think of any other greeting.

"I am a Watcher," the child said.

"Yeah. So I've been told. So what have you seen? Can you tell me where to go?"

The child seemed to hesitate. "You can't do anything," he said. "The battle is beyond you."

"But I have to try to fight it," Chris said. "For love. Do you get that?"

"I can show you one thing," the child said.

"Then show me. Please."

The child held up his hand, and Chris saw:

Not what he expected to see. Not Reese, not Miranda, not the old man who had been Clint.

He saw Tyler.

In the city below.

Chris came out of nowhere and grabbed Tyler in a hug, and then practically threw him against the wall of the nearest building under the streetlights and said, "Where are they?"

"I don't know where you just came from, but I'm really happy to see you," Tyler said.

"You too," Chris said, and despite the shortness of the words, his eyes said he meant it. "I don't think we have a lot of time. Where are they?"

"I assume you mean Jacob and Reese, and you're right, we don't. They're heading for a cemetery."

"And you aren't with them because . . ."

"It's a long story." Tyler's eyes went to the man standing behind Chris, whose expression was somewhere between curiosity and nervous breakdown.

"Andrew Hunter," Chris said. "He's Miranda's father. Julie's husband."

"Oh," Tyler said. "Listen, I'm sorry about what happened to her."

"What happened to her didn't," Chris said. "Well, it did, but she's alive."

"What are you talking about?"

"Let's just say there's something to all this Spirit stuff." Chris's eyes were dangerous. "Do you know where this cemetery is?"

"Yes. I just need a car to get there. I hitchhiked this far."

"Come on, then," Chris said. "Let's go."

*　*　*　*　*

Reese and Jacob left the car a mile from the cemetery and walked the rest of the way, creeping through the darkness closer and closer to the place where Jacob had spent the most haunted, tormented years of his younger life—the years after his wife's death and the persecution of the Oneness that had left so many dead, wounded, and bereft. It was here, in the midst of the gravestones where he'd believed Bertoller to be buried, that he had experienced his greatest epiphany: that he could not fulfil his calling as Oneness, could make no real difference in the world, could combat the darkness not at all, if he was not willing to bring justice to the true vessels of evil in the world.

To men like Franz Bertoller.

Reese had been here only once before, but as they drew closer, through the dry grass and weeds buzzing with night insects, she felt something of the strange mix of apprehension, memory, and excitement Jacob felt—of all the places Jacob had shown her, of all the arguments he had levelled, it was the one encapsulated here that had most shaken her.

The insects stopped buzzing within a quarter mile of the cemetery. They went on in absolute silence, the only sounds those they made themselves—breathing, rustling in the weeds. Reese could hear her own heartbeat and suspected she could hear Jacob's also.

A growing pressure in her ears alerted her to the presence of the invisible. Her entourage—the powers she had called upon to bring her this far. Jacob could feel them too. He was pleased they were there.

She didn't know how she felt about it. Only that this man had to be stopped. Just had to be.

Nothing else would be good enough.

And if David was involved . . .

He could not be allowed to become another Bertoller.

* * * * *

A motorcycle growling up to the road to the cemetery came, bearing the last sacrifice not a minute early.

Bertoller had spent the last half hour cursing the lateness of their arrival. He badly wanted to get this over with.

When his hired man appeared in the torchlight leading another man, this one with his hands bound and his eyes blindfolded, Bertoller saw April cast him a look of question and deep concern.

As if he would answer her.

But he wanted her to know who this man was, so for effect, he said, "Welcome, David. I'm so glad you could be part of this after all."

David spat out his response. "Bertoller! You backstabbing son of the devil! You don't dare kill me!"

"Give me one reason why I would be afraid to do that," Bertoller said, glad for the diversion the man provided. "Because you're Oneness? I have spent most of my life battling the Oneness—and you hardly deserve to be lumped in among them. Because . . . hmm. I can't think of a single other possible reason."

"We had plans together," David sputtered. "We were partners."

"Yes, and the partnership ended when you failed utterly to fulfil your purpose in it."

"I can still give you access to the Oneness," David said, his words beginning to falter now. "You still need that. To infect the—"

"I have other access points now. Far more powerful ones. You've heard of Reese? Jacob? It turns out they've both given into the darkness more fully than I could have hoped."

"How could you even know . . ."

"The demonic has ears everywhere. My power is not so diminished that I don't know how to listen."

"I gave you Reese," David said. His tone was pathetic now—he had ceased threatening, ceased bargaining; this was nothing more than a plaintive whine.

"Your usefulness is done. Except for what you will provide as fuel for the fire." Bertoller nodded to the man. "Chain him up with the woman."

"No!" David said, trying to jerk away from his captor but to no avail. "No! I won't die alongside her! I won't be one of them!"

"You cannot help that," Bertoller said. "The only grip in this universe stronger than that of the demonic is that of the Spirit, I'm sorry to say. And you will never wriggle loose of that grip."

David was taken across the clearing and bound beside April, whose head was bowed. Bertoller half-expected her to say something—some cloying, sympathetic thing. She didn't. Not a word.

He found that unnerving but did all in his power not to show that.

He would give anything to know what had happened to her between her first capture on this day and the second. Something had altered her—had altered everything. Something had changed her so deeply that it had taken this entire night out of his hands and made it a wild card.

He didn't know what was going to happen when he began the sacrifice.

He quickly shut down that train of thought, only momentarily entertaining the idea of torturing her to force her to tell him what had happened.

That too was quickly dismissed.

He had a terrible sense that she would tell him, and the knowledge would make things more unpredictable than they already were.

Forcing his hand steady, he picked up a crooked knife, stood on the gravestone he'd been using as a dais, and said in a tightly controlled voice, "Let all who are not sanctified leave this place."

The response was most of the men—only four had gone through the necessary rites. Only four wanted power other than money. Only four were willing to face the darkness and invite the demonic fully.

Under normal circumstances, Bertoller would have commended them for doing what he had done many years ago and never regretted.

Tonight, he wasn't certain their choice would prove to be a good one.

What was happening to him?

The girl, Miranda, was starting to cry again—to whine and blubber. It would feel good to quiet her permanently. Her cries snapped him out of his paralysis. The hour was approaching. The sickle moon was high overhead.

It was time.

* * * * *

Visions dogged Reese as they drew close enough to the cemetery to see light—torchlight. They tormented her. She saw it over and over again: Jacob being shot. Chris being shot. Tyler sacrificed. David satisfied.

David smiling.

David free.

She saw Jacob shot down, point-blank, Bertoller holding the gun.

She saw a spray of bullets take Chris down.

She saw Miranda . . .

The visions were interrupted by an exodus of men from the cemetery, coming through the grass. One roared by on a motorcycle. Jacob saw them before she did and yanked her aside, the two of them hunkering down in the long weeds and hoping no one would trip over them.

She hoped Tyler was praying.

She wondered when she had lost the ability to pray.

When she had stopped trusting the Spirit to hear, or act, or care at all.

A sound was coming from the cemetery—unsettling, grating. It took her a moment to recognize it.

It was crying.

Hysterics, really.

A young woman or a child.

She closed her eyes and tightened her grip on the hunting knife in her hands.

Miranda.

The men had passed; it did not sound as though anyone else was coming their way. Jacob motioned for her to stay down and rose warily. They were within feet of the iron fence around the cemetery now, and keeping in the shadows of a row of trees, Jacob maneuvered closer.

Reese watched him, watched the dancing shadows, watched the moonlight and listened to Miranda crying.

Her heart beat out urgency: Get in there. Stop him. Save her. Save them.

Kill him.

It's the only way.

Jacob reappeared beside her—it was amazing how quickly he could move. "It's a ritual," he said. "A sacrifice. He's got . . ."

His voice trailed away.

"Miranda," Reese finished.

He nodded. But he wasn't telling her everything.

"And?"

"And others."

"Who?"

"I don't know the woman," Jacob said. "A young woman. Blonde."

"April," Reese said, sure of it. She had been their target before. It made sense.

"Remember, Reese," Jacob said, his voice so quiet it was barely audible, "stay focused. Go for Bertoller. Only Bertoller. No matter what. You take him down, you've defeated the worst evil our world has known in centuries."

She nodded and flexed her fingers around the knife again. Even now, surrounded by demons, barely recognizable to herself as Oneness, she hated the thought of killing a man.

Even this man.

Maybe she would pretend he was David, and let her pain and confusion drive the knife home.

Maybe she would simply get revenge.

"No matter what, Reese," Jacob said again.

"Yes," she answered, irritated now. "I understand."

* * * * *

There was a set order to the ritual.

It was supposed to begin with animal sacrifices, and that was to be followed by the preliminary human sacrifices—the girl and David.

It would culminate in the death of the great saint. And Bertoller and his lackeys would drink in the pleasure of the Power, and his spirit would fill their veins and flood their bodies.

He couldn't follow the protocol.

He ran through the liturgy, the opening rites, but with every word the pressure grew—a deep inner panic growing by the moment. Either the woman was far stronger, or he was far weaker, than he had understood until now.

Eyes. He could feel eyes everywhere. Watching. Witnessing. Judging.

He was going mad.

The torches flared.

The moon glared down, waxing before his very eyes, growing stronger, rounder, a great eye.

The goats bleated and the girl-child cried.

His lackeys, cloaked in black, were going about the rites as he had taught them to do: going to the animals.

"No!" he shrieked.

He froze. His heart beating in his ears. They turned and queried silently, surprised as he was.

"Leave them," he said. "Bring the woman."

One of them dared question him. "But—"

"NOW!"

He wanted to watch them, but he couldn't. If he did his eyes would fall on April, and he could not look at her.

He turned his back, wrestling, trying to slow his heartbeat, calm his voice, get back into control.

The eye of the moon stared down.

He heard the chains and the noise as they brought the woman to the pyre. There was a stake there, a shorter one, and they would chain her to it and burn her alive.

He gathered his wits and turned.

But the woman he saw was not April.

It was Teresa.

For a moment the breath was gone from his lungs.

She looked like she had six hundred years ago—hair long and dark, skin like cream, eyes dark. Her whole bearing holiness.

And her eyes full of compassion.

They were still full of compassion.

He had not thought he would ever see her again.

"You were wrong," she said.

"No," he tried to say, but his mouth was dry as the kindling, and he could not speak.

He kept hoping she would disappear, but every time he blinked, he opened his eyes again and she was still there. Standing in front of the pyre. His men were working behind her; April was there, but Teresa stood in his line of vision.

*　*　*　*　*

April could not tear her eyes away from Bertoller.

He seemed to have aged, even in the time since she entered the cemetery. Looking at him, she saw a man ancient and withered, hardly alive. But his eyes were tormented, and it was that that riveted her attention.

He was not dead.

He was not beyond reach.

Even this man had a soul.

She had always known that. The Oneness taught it—she'd heard it from Mary a thousand times. Every human being is a soul. Every human being needs saving, and is worth saving. Every one.

But she wouldn't have believed it was true of this one, if she couldn't see it with her own eyes.

She wasn't afraid. She didn't really know why. She stood in

the midst of kindling with her hands chained to a stake, and she knew perfectly well what these men were planning to do with her. She was going to be sacrificed to the darkness to feed their lust for power.

But it was all going as she had warned Bertoller it would—even now, before they had finished the work. It was backfiring on them. On him. Something was waking his soul.

Miranda was crying, and that one detail tugged at her heart and broke through the strange, almost emotionless detachment she felt toward their circumstances. That, and David. Still tied to the first stake a small distance away, he was a pillar of rage and fear.

She wanted to give them what she had: the fearlessness that came of knowledge. Of knowing the Spirit.

But she couldn't just give that.

They had to find it for themselves.

So she said the most natural thing she could say.

"Spirit," she said, aloud. "Come." She paused, and felt that the next words came from beyond her somewhere.

"I offer myself to you."

* * * * *

The cloaked acolyte handed Bertoller a burning torch, his eyes questioning the change in liturgy but his actions still obedient. After all, Bertoller was the master. The one showing them the way.

The only one who could invite the Power itself into their presence and give them all to drink of its cup.

Bertoller took the torch, and as he did, Teresa faded from his vision.

Deep inside him, something cried out with grief at the loss. Reached out . . .

He cut it off, fixing his eyes on April, setting his mind to the task and the reward to come.

Power. Life. The drunkenness of the demonic. All he needed to do was honour the Power as he ended the life of this enemy in torment.

He began the slow, ceremonious walk forward.

And nearly dropped the torch.

Before his eyes—

—before all their eyes—

smoke was already rising from the pyre.

Smoke, and then flame.

Before Bertoller had taken another step, the sacrifice burst into flames. He watched as fire licked up the kindling and swallowed April in a blaze of heat. The roar of it filled the cemetery, filled the night, reached the moon.

* * * * *

"No!" Reese cried, even as Jacob cried "Now!" and shoved her forward. Her legs were already going. She vaulted the fence and ran toward the fire, the light, the place where she knew Bertoller was standing. The knife in her hand seemed welded to her.

The demon voices in her ears were shouting.

ONE TASK.

FOCUS.

STAY FOCUSED.

Bertoller saw her coming, and his eyes widened.

There were tears in his eyes.

And David was there behind him.

Her momentum might have carried her right to him, and the knife right through his heart, if the pyre had not exploded, a ball of flame surging out in every direction, the heat knocking her off her feet. Off course. Off focus.

Fire everywhere.

Everything was on fire.

In the midst, on the pyre, April was standing with her hands held high. Glowing like gold in a furnace.

Oh Reese, Reese, Reese, where have you gone?

The voice was the fire and the fire was the voice, and it burned—it burned to the depths of her soul and spirit, and she screamed at the heat and released it all in the scream.

One thing.

One task.

She saw Jacob running into the flames, looking wildly around. She heard Miranda scream his name, scream for help.

There was another explosion coming—she could see it. It was building up around April, the fire growing hotter and whiter, April herself transformed into something that was not human—at least, that was not human in any way Reese understood the word.

She dropped the knife and ran for David and threw herself around him, and when the explosion came, she took it.

* * * * *

"NO!"

The word came from Chris and Andrew at the same moment, and as one they broke into a run, pounding the dirt toward the cemetery, calling out the names on their hearts—

"Miranda!"

"Reese!"

"STOP!" Tyler tackled Chris from behind and managed to trip Andrew in the same moment. "Stop," he panted, "you can't go in there!"

Andrew turned frantic eyes on him even as he scrambled back to his feet. "That's my kid in there!"

"You can't help her! Listen to me. That's not an ordinary fire. I can see it. It's not just fire, it's . . . please, stay here."

Andrew shook his head and went to run again, but this time Chris stopped him, wrapping strong arms around him and wrestling him back.

"Listen to Tyler. He knows."

They stood ten feet from the cemetery gates and stared into the inferno. Its roar had covered every other sound.

"Tyler . . ." Chris said. "What . . ."

"It's the Spirit," Tyler said. His voice shook. "The fire. It's the Spirit."

From the inferno, figures were taking shape. Golden, shining, outlined in the flames.

Three women.

They were coming, and Chris found himself slowly dropping to his knees. Andrew followed suit. Only Tyler remained on his feet, but seconds before the figures stepped out of the flames, he smiled suddenly and knelt beside the others. And bowed his head.

Chris looked up.

April stood there, every inch herself—and every inch transformed. She was glowing. She was holding Miranda's hand.

On her other side stood a woman Chris didn't know. Her hair was long and dark; she wore white, a simple dress that looked as though it came from another era.

Andrew choked up and reached his hands forward, self-conscious. "My girl," he said, his eyes fixed on Miranda. "Miranda."

Miranda just stared at him, but April nudged her forward. "You can go to him," she said. "He's safe."

She exchanged glances with the woman beside her, and the dark-haired woman nodded and smiled.

And faded from sight.

The fire still raged behind them.

And Chris's heart broke.

Reese had not emerged from the fire.

* * * * *

In the hours that the fire raged, Andrew took Miranda away. He had introduced himself, and she seemed strangely open to him—or just relieved to be able to escape. They were going to find some food, Andrew told Chris, to find some twenty-four-hour diner somewhere.

Chris just nodded.

Still staring into the fire.

Tyler and April disappeared somewhere. He didn't know where.

He didn't care.

How a fire could burn so strong, so long, he didn't know. He couldn't go closer. The heat was too great. Sparks rose and flames danced and the air filled with smoke until the moon and the stars disappeared.

And Chris sat in the grass and waited.

"I'm sorry, Reese," he said. "I'm sorry I didn't do more to find you. I'm sorry I didn't try to bring you home—that I didn't become One with you. If I had, maybe you would have reconnected. Maybe . . ."

He stopped.

He couldn't go on.

When he thought about it now, he didn't know why he hadn't opened himself to the Spirit and become One.

Maybe he'd thought that if he did, and Reese came to love him, it wouldn't be because of him. That he would lose himself in the Oneness. Lose his will, his strength, his personhood.

He wasn't afraid of that now.

Because staring into this fire that was Spirit, he knew it wasn't true.

That this fire refined. It did not muddy down.

Hours passed. Hours of heat and light until he wondered if his vision would be forever burned away.

"I don't care anymore," he said. "If you're still watching me, you know that . . . you can have me. I need you."

He paused.

"I've always needed you."

When the sun rose, the fire died away. It left the cemetery a smoking, barren field, the headstones unreadable from soot, every last bit of grass and foliage burned away.

Chris wondered what it had found to feed on so long.

Tyler stood—Chris wasn't sure when he had come back— but Chris didn't acknowledge him. He walked through the gate into the smoking ground. He looked back just long enough to see April stop Tyler at the gate, and the two of them waiting—watching.

He turned away, wished he could steel himself with a deep breath but hardly able to breathe at all in the ash and smoke, and pressed further into the cemetery.

He knew there had been human beings here last night, but there was no trace of them. They had been consumed in the flame.

Bertoller, gone forever.

Jacob too.

The thoughts passed through his mind but hardly registered.

Reese . . .

He could not even form that thought.

He licked his lips. They were cracked and blistered. His whole face was cracked and blistered—he'd sat closer to the fire than he'd realized.

Smoke wafted in pillars and plumes, and yet, somehow, the air felt purified.

He looked to the side and saw the child, watching.

He raised his hand in greeting and dropped it again, setting his eyes forward once more.

And then he saw it.

An ashy mound on the slab headstone in the middle of the cemetery—

A mound that looked like bodies.

Clenching his jaw, he forced one foot after the other until he was looking down, unbelieving.

It was Reese. Covered in ash. Lying over top of someone else.

His hand was shaking as he reached out and touched her shoulder.

She moved. Rolled over. Looked up at him with her eyes open.

"Reese," he said.

The man beside her groaned, and involuntarily, Chris's eyes went to him. He took a step back as if he'd been shot.

David.

The man was David.

Reese sat up, slowly, starting to brush herself off and then giving up in futility. She rubbed her hands together to clean off as much ash as she could and then tried to clean her face. And she looked up at Chris and smiled.

Really smiled.

Not the broken, halfhearted, trying-to-believe-again smile that was all he knew from her.

He wasn't sure which of them moved first, but she was in his arms a moment later, and he was holding her as tightly as he could, his arms sure they would never let go.

The windows were all thrown open, letting in a warm late summer breeze, and Melissa's music—celebratory, triumphant music—played out so all the neighbourhood could hear. Ordinary mortals might not understand what the cell was celebrating so heartily, but they could not miss the party.

In the common room, in front of the fireplace, Chris's arms were wrapped around Reese. She sat with her head resting on his chest, her favourite place to be.

They were One. And openly in love.

Chris was still trying to get used to the idea that Reese was alive.

Richard smiled down at them and escorted April from the room, leaving them alone except for Melissa at the piano—and as she was in her own world there, they hardly felt the company.

Chris leaned his head on Reese's, and they simply sat together.

Replaying her memories, as much as she had shared them with him.

Andrew and Miranda were in the kitchen, talking happily with Mary and Diane. Nick and Alicia ran through the common room, throwing curious glances at Reese and Chris, who ignored them completely.

The day before, they had gone together to return David to the police.

"And where is Jacob?" Lieutenant Jackson asked, accepting David's return almost with bewilderment. He had been missing only a few hours.

"I'm afraid he's not coming back," Chris said.

"The devil he isn't!"

"He's dead," Reese said. "I'm sorry. He ran into a fire to—to save someone. He didn't make it."

"You expect me to put that on my paperwork?"

"It's the truth," Chris said.

"Like that has anything to do with it."

When they left, Chris said, "Are you going to tell me what really happened to Jacob?"

Reese was quiet for a moment, then she took Chris's arm and said, "He tried to kill Bertoller. It almost seemed like he might make it—like the flames might not destroy him, the way they didn't hurt April. But Miranda called for him, and instead of helping her, he went after Bertoller to murder him. The fire consumed them both."

"I'm not sure I understand how Miranda made it out. She's not One."

"But she's innocent. And April protected her."

"Like you did David."

"A little differently."

"Why did you do it? Throw yourself over David? Keep him safe from the flames all that time?"

"Because I knew they would destroy him. Like they did Jacob. And . . ."

She stopped and clung a little more tightly. "Chris, I don't expect you to understand. But I loved David. He was my brother—more like a father. Like Richard is to Tyler and April and the others. I had forgotten that, almost. Let bitterness choke it out. And listened to lies. The demons told me David was there when Patrick was killed. Maybe he was. But maybe he wasn't. They 'showed' me a lot of things that weren't true."

"It's okay, Reese," Chris said. "Anyone who went through what you did . . ."

"It's not okay. Not really. I almost forgot what Oneness is. I almost killed a man. I thought I had the right to judge him. But judgment is easy. Killing is sudden, and final. Redemption is a far longer work. It is that work we are here to do. I should never have lost sight of that."

"I still don't understand what changed your heart in the last minute. From what you told me, you went into the cemetery ready to kill them both."

"I did." Reese stopped and sat on a park bench, still clinging to Chris's hand. She had gone from independent to desperate to hang on to him, almost as though she was afraid to be left alone.

He didn't mind. He didn't want to leave her anyway.

"I don't know what changed me. Don't credit me with that much understanding of my own heart. It may have been the flames themselves. The refiner's fire . . . they may have simply burned the bitterness away. But there was something else."

"Tell me."

"Bertoller. I saw something in his eyes. He had a soul . . . and I think, somehow, he had just rediscovered it." Her voice dropped almost to a whisper. "I know he earned his death a million times over. But I wish he could have made it—could have been allowed to rediscover his soul completely."

"Hush," Chris said. "That was never for you to decide."

He pulled her close.

Happy, at last.

One, at last.

The renegade had finally come home.

* * * * *

The story continues in Book 5: RISE.

Rachel would love to hear from you!

You can visit her and interact online:
Web: **www.rachelstarrthomson.com**
Facebook: **www.facebook.com/RachelStarrThomsonWriter**
Twitter: **@writerstarr**

THE SEVENTH WORLD TRILOGY

Worlds Unseen   Burning Light   Coming Day

For five hundred years the Seventh World has been ruled by a tyrannical empire—and the mysterious Order of the Spider that hides in its shadow. History and truth are deliberately buried, the beauty and treachery of the past remembered only by wandering Gypsies, persecuted scholars, and a few unusual seekers. But the past matters, as Maggie Sheffield soon finds out. It matters because its forces will soon return and claim lordship over her world, for good or evil.

The Seventh World Trilogy is an epic fantasy, beautiful, terrifying, pointing to the realities just beyond the world we see.

"An excellent read, solidly recommended for fantasy readers."
– Midwest Book Review

"A wonderfully realistic fantasy world. Recommended."
– Jill Williamson, Christy-Award-Winning Author
of *By Darkness Hid*

"Epic, beautiful, well-written fantasy that sings of Christian truth."
– Rael, reader

Available everywhere online or special order from your local bookstore.

THE ONENESS CYCLE

Exile   Hive   Attack   Renegade   Rise

The supernatural entity called the Oneness holds the world together.
What happens if it falls apart?

In a world where the Oneness exists, nothing looks the same. Dead men walk. Demons prowl the air. Old friends peel back their mundane masks and prove as supernatural as angels. But after centuries of battling demons and the corrupting powers of the world, the Oneness is under a new threat—its greatest threat. Because this time, the threat comes from within.

Fast-paced contemporary fantasy.

"Plot twists and lots of edge-of-your-seat action,
I had a hard time putting it down!"
—Alexis

"Finally! The kind of fiction I've been waiting for my whole life!"
—Mercy Hope, FaithTalks.com

"I sped through this short, fast-paced novel, pleased by the well-drawn characters and the surprising plot. Thomson has done a great job of portraying difficult emotional journeys . . . Read it!"
—Phyllis Wheeler, The Christian Fantasy Review

Available everywhere online or special order from your local bookstore.

TAERITH

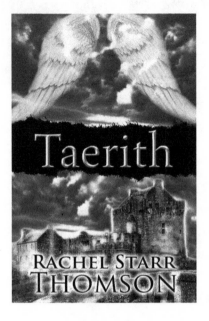

When he rescues a young woman named Lilia from bandits, Taerith Romany is caught in a web of loyalties: Lilia is the future queen of a spoiled king, and though Taerith is not allowed to love her, neither he can bring himself to leave her without a friend. Their lives soon intertwine with the fiercely proud slave girl, Mirian, whose tragic past and wild beauty make her the target of the king's unscrupulous brother.

The king's rule is only a knife's edge from slipping—and when it does, all three will be put to the ultimate test. In a land of fog and fens, unicorns and wild men, Taerith stands at the crossroads of good and evil, where men are vanquished by their own obsessions or saved by faith in higher things.

"Devastatingly beautiful . . . I am amazed at every chapter how deeply you've caused us to care for these characters."
—Gabi

"Deeply satisfying." —Kapezia

"Rachel Starr Thomson is an artist, and every chapter of Taerith is like a painting . . . beautiful."
—Brittany Simmons

Available everywhere online or special order from your local bookstore.

ANGEL IN THE WOODS

Hawk is a would-be hero in search of a giant to kill or a maiden to save. The trouble is, when he finds them, there are forty-some maidens—and they call their giant "the Angel." Before he knows what's happening, Hawk is swept into the heart of a patchwork family and all of its mysteries, carried away by their camaraderie—and falling quickly in love.

But the outside world cannot be kept at bay forever. Suspecting the Giant of hiding a treasure, the wealthy and influential Widow Brawnlyn sets out to tear the family apart and bring the Giant to destruction any way she can. And her two principle weapons are Hawk—and the truth.

Caught between the terrible truths he discovers about the family's past and the unalterable fact that he has come to love them, Hawk must face his fears and overcome his flaws if he is to rescue the Angel in the woods.

"A beautiful tale of finding oneself, honor and heroism; a story I will not soon forget." — Szoch

"The more I think about it, the more truth and beauty I find in the story." —H. A. Titus

Available everywhere online or special order from your local bookstore.

REAP THE WHIRLWIND

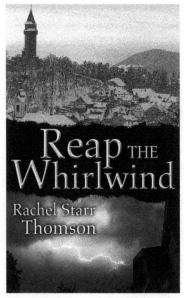

Beren is a city in constant unrest: ruled by a ruthless upper class and harried by a band of rebels who want change. Its one certainty is that the two sides do not, and will not, meet.

But children know little of sides or politics, and Anna and Kyara—a princess and a peasant girl—let their chance meeting grow into a deep friendship. Until the day Kyara's family is slaughtered by Anna's people, and the friendship comes to an abrupt end.

Years later, Kyara is a rebel—bitter, hard, and violent. Anna's efforts to fight the political system she belongs to avail little. Neither is a child anymore—but neither has ever forgotten the power of their long-ago friendship. When a secret plot brings the rebellion to a fiery head, both young women know it is too late to save the land they love.

But is it too late to save each other?

Available everywhere online.

LADY MOON

When Celine meets Tomas, they are in a cavern on the moon where she has been languishing for thirty days after being banished by her evil uncle for throwing a scrub brush at his head. Tomas is a charming and eccentric Immortal, hanging out on the moon because he's procrastinating his destiny—meeting, and defeating, Celine's uncle.

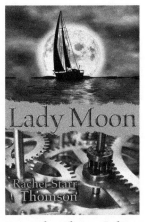

A pair of magic rings send them back to earth, where Celine insists on returning home and is promptly thrown into the dungeon. Her uncle, Ignus Umbria, is up to no good, and his latest caper threatens to devour the whole countryside. He doesn't want Celine getting in the way. More than that, he wants to force Tomas into a confrontation—and Tomas, who has fallen in love with Celine, cannot procrastinate any longer.

Lady Moon is a fast-paced, humorous adventure in a world populated by mad magicians, walking rosebushes, thieving scullery maids, and other improbable things. And of course, the most improbable—and magical—thing of all: true love.

"Celine's sarcastic 'languishing' immediately put me in mind of Patricia C. Wrede's Dealing with Dragons series—a fairy tale that gently makes fun of the usual fairy tale tropes. And once again, Rachel Starr Thomson doesn't disappoint."

— H. A. Titus

"Funny and quirky fantasy."

Available everywhere online.

Short Fiction by Rachel Starr Thomson

BUTTERFLIES DANCING

FALLEN STAR

OF MEN AND BONES

OGRES IS

JOURNEY

MAGDALENE

THE CITY CAME CREEPING

WAYFARER'S DREAM

WAR WITH THE MUSE

SHIELDS OF THE EARTH

And more!

*Available as downloads for
Kindle, Kobo, Nook, iPad, and more!*

CPSIA information can be obtained
at www.ICGtesting.com
Printed in the USA
LVHW04s2347160818
587183LV00004B/267/P